DECCAN QUEEN

Take Two

FARRUKH DHONDY

Om Books International

First published in 2024 by

Om Books International

Corporate & Editorial Office
A-12, Sector 64, Noida 201 301
Uttar Pradesh, India
Phone: +91 120 477 4100
Email: editorial@ombooks.com
Website: www.ombooksinternational.com

Sales Office
107, Ansari Road, Darya Ganj,
New Delhi 110 002, India
Phone: +91 11 4000 9000
Email: sales@ombooks.com
Website: www.ombooks.com

ISBN: 978-93-5376-975-8

Printed in India

10 9 8 7 6 5 4 3 2 1

DECCAN QUEEN

Take Two

Farrukh Dhondy was born in 1944 in Pune, India. He went to school and college in Pune and then won a scholarship to Cambridge University, UK, where he graduated with a dual degree in Quantum Physics and English. He went on to write several books, among them *The Bikini Murders* and his autobiography, *Fragments Against My Ruin*. He has written TV sitcoms including *Tandoori Nights* and famous screenplays, among them *Bandit Queen, Mangal Pandey* and *Jinnah*. He has also written stage plays and is a regular columnist for several newspapers. He lives in Britain and has been a political activist and a commissioning editor on Channel 4 UK TV.

Praise for Farrukh Dhondy

"In *Bombay Duck*, Farrukh Dhondy amazingly manages to ladle out a marvellous send-up of the fraud bazaar that makes for cultural internationalism."

—*India Today*

"...the final kicker in the last paragraph [of *The Bikini Murders*] is one that knocks your socks off. It's worth every page of the rest of the book, because even if you're the kind who can't resist peeking at the end, you won't make sense of it without reading what went before. Just hang in there. You'll be rewarded. Guaranteed."

—*India Today*

"There are reasons why [*Fragments Against My Ruin*] stands out against standard autobiographical fares. Firstly, the literary quality that informs every page of the work in a language that is precise and witty. Secondly, Dhondy exhibits a rare degree of frankness in revealing himself, as also others, eminent and ordinary, observed through his acute mind."

—*The Tribune*

"If adultery is like a shadow to an individual, shifty and unshakeable, that socio-moral theme finds its reflection in the literary form. Every story [in *Adultery and Other Stories*] has an overt, regular narrative, and a shadowy adulterous sub-narrative. Some very adult tales, told with childlike ease."

—*Hindustan Times*

"Dhondy has one sterling quality and that is an unflinching, ruthless honesty. If you want to know whence love, and whither, [*Adultery and Other Stories*] is a pretty good map."

—*DNA*

"Transcendent yet simple, Rumi's words—in this exquisite translation by Farrukh Dhondy—forever remain the anchor of the human condition."

—Mira Nair on Dhondy's first selection of translations from Rumi's works, *Rumi: A New Translation*

"Multi-layered, challenging and filled with mysterious beauty, this quirky novel [*Black Swan*] will provide a rare treat for sophisticated readers ... the contemporary story lines are utterly engrossing ... Dhondy's pulse-quickening novel makes crystal-clear the revolutionary power of the written and the spoken word."

—*Publisher's Weekly*

To my cousins the Modys, Mehtas, Antias and Dhondys with whom I lived through the years on which this fiction is based

Contents

Preface

Dear readers, I don't know how many of you read the first edition of this concatenation of experiences—or shall I call them "stories", putting them firmly in the category of fiction. At any rate, some readers went through that first edition and, even though I had been very diligent in altering or disguising the names of the characters who featured in those pieces, fancied that they had been libelled, parodied, falsely represented in untrue circumstances and generally brought into disrepute.

They wrote back, some in unpleasant terms, others furiously and still others in ways that were, I felt, importuning.

I am not going to admit here—or in any court of law—that these individuals have correctly identified themselves as the people I have characterized or used dramatically in these stories!

There you are: I am insisting that their objections have no basis, and I beg to put the obvious questions to them and to the readers of this second edition or second "take".

What the hell is fiction anyway? What is its relation to things that have happened or could have happened? Even in the realistic genre, is there a distinction between the truth and the fictional truth?

I pose these questions but can't answer them, however important they are. Of course, I believe the answers to these questions are keys to dimensions in our imaginations. Even in civilization. How true is a "story"? (I could go further and, without the least claim to contributing to, or my efforts being classified as such, ask, "How true is literature?")

In the search for an answer to the former question and in an act of fairness and generosity—let's leave "literature" out of it—this second "take" has at the end of each of its sections or "stories" the precise objections that the people who identified themselves as the libelled or offended characters submitted to the publisher, to me and perhaps to their lawyers.

I am not in the least anxious about answering an allegation arising from these objections in court. I even hope that giving the objections to my "stories" an airing in this "second edition" will act, not as an apology, but as a balancing act.

So, dear readers, you have before you *Deccan Queen Take Two*.

A Maharaja's Ransom

My grandfather used to sing in the bath. It wasn't really a bath. It was a room with one corner of it paved with flagstones and the paved section enclosed by two parapets, one low enough to climb over into the bathing space and the other waist-high to shut off the wet area from the dry. There was a single cold-water tap, and buckets of scalding water, heated on a wood-burning stove, were brought from the kitchen to make up the tepid bath water. In the corner of this *mori* there was a hole with a metal grill for the waste to run into. That's where we, a crew of siblings and cousins below the age of four, believed the demons lived. In all the holes in the floor of this decaying mansion, the last house in Khambatta Gully, Byculla, Bombay, grandiosely named Dhondy Terrace, we intuited demons.

Dhondy Terrace had pseudo Art Nouveau wrought-iron balconies and mosaic floors. I was two-and-a-half years old. I was my grandfather's companion, and he took me for walks and told me stories. I didn't know it at the time but the stories were an anthology of Greek myths, tales from the Ramayana and Mahabharata, the story of Rustom and Sohrab and a hundred others.

By all accounts my grandfather was an accomplished and literate man, fluent in Urdu and Persian and something of an expert on Persian poetry. I don't think he knew Sanskrit, though there were books and manuscripts in that language that remained in the family archive, such as it was.

My grandfather, Khurshedji, had inherited lands, estates and houses in several towns and territories of the Raj's Western Presidency, around Bombay and in a town further north called Deolali in which there was even a road named after our family.

Khurshedji was the eldest of four brothers, two of whom had left the joint family household and moved out. The first one to leave had taken up medicine as a profession, had joined the army and married a lady who wanted to live in a style more elevated than that of the Parsi joint family into which she had married. She was always accused of causing the first breach. She had illusions of being like the British memsahibs, the wives of my granduncle's fellow officers in the British Indian army.

The youngest brother, Rustom, Russi, a Gandhian by conviction, had left home and moved into his wife's old-fashioned, dark but sumptuously large mansion and had inherited from his father a factory that manufactured industrial soap. To the two older brothers then, the building trade and the reputation of Master Builders and to the youngest son, the soap.

My great-grandfather had brought his family to Bombay, made his fortune there and, immersing himself in the enterprise that was the spirit of nascent Bombay, invested in an industrial soap factory, which then grew from being a shed with woodfires boiling animal fat and oil in large vats stirred by sweated labour into a small mill with oil-powered, paddled machines to do the stirring and metal casts in which the cakes of soap solidified.

The Diana Soap factory and its success brought him to the attention of a British civil service grandee of the time who, impressed with the progress of my great-grandfather's personal hand and determination in converting a sweatshop shed into a factory, encouraged him to start a small building business and gave him government contracts to get him going.

Bombay was undergoing its late nineteenth-century industry and building boom. Ships from London, Southampton, Liverpool, Leith and Glasgow and from other more exotic places that were clients of the British Empire, harboured in the bay. The swamp and sea between the seven islands were being reclaimed as land, with cartloads of mud and rock displacing the shallow's slush. The peninsula that was to be thus integrated and become Bombay was well on the way to becoming the metropolis of western India.

It was this building business that my grandfather had inherited from his father. He set about as a young man expanding it, hiring young Parsi civil engineers, architects trained in England and Germany and gangs of labourers who came from the villages into the city looking for work.

He grew rich and befriended the Jamsaheb, Maharaja of Jamnagar, through their mutual love of polo. Khurshedji, my grandfather, was reputed to have kept a fine stable of polo ponies. The Raja had a retinue, and the friends would eat, drink and travel the country in carriages together. They sailed to Paris and London on an eight-month cruise. And all the while, the joint family was amassing a small fortune, buying more property and building for governments and kings.

One drunken evening, Jamsaheb, sitting in his palace in the capital Jamnagar, turned to Khurshedji and said, "This kingdom needs a hospital and a university. Build me both."

Khurshedji is said to have replied that a friend's wish was his command, and the next day the lands were allocated and work began. No cost was spared. The most famous architects from Europe were contracted, marble and stone were imported, artworks and scientific laboratories to rival those of Cambridge were commissioned. As the months progressed so did the buildings. The university with its vast gardens and the hospital with its spacious wards, an art-nouveau frontage and gothic towers, became the pride of the town.

The buildings were nearly complete when Jamsaheb fell off his polo horse and was trampled to death. His eldest widow, who had from the day she was married to Jamsaheb resented my grandfather as the influence that was leading him to drink, to the pleasures of dancing girls in the court and to Paris and London, was appointed regent for her twelve-year-old son.

Khurshedji had no written contracts for the buildings and now owed lakhs or even crores of rupees to the sub-contractors, suppliers and his work force. He had counted on the money coming in as it would most certainly have if Jamsaheb had lived. He approached the Queen-regent who smiled and turned him away. What money was he talking about? Surely the buildings had been paid for?

To which court would he appeal? The British Agent resident in Kirtinagar knew the whole story, and sided with Khurshedji in sentiment, but was powerless to intervene. Larger political considerations of the Raj meant that the Queen-regent had to be kept loyal to the British Raj administration still in Calcutta.

My grandfather's brothers, one who worked with him and one who had kept his dormant share in the business while enlisting in the King's Indian army, fell upon him, securing their own possessions and positions by demanding that the lands and buildings they jointly owned be transferred to them so as to avoid the creditors getting hold of them. As my father told the story, his father was an honourable man and didn't want to defraud his creditors by declaring himself bankrupt. He agreed to a division of the properties with his brothers, handed his own share over to the courts of the British Raj in which he and his building firm were being sued for settlement of debts and declared himself a pauper, unable to pay. Bankruptcy was unavoidable.

It all went: the polo ponies, the estates, the grand houses down the road named after our family, a family not of proud Parsi aristocracy now but of a foolish and disgraced bankrupt.

My father and his sisters lost their servants, attendants, country resorts and beach bungalows and were withdrawn from their expensive hill-station boarding schools and sent to the newly established Parsi Orphanage for the poor of the community.

My grandfather, a broken man, lived off the meagre charity afforded him by his brothers and spent his time attending the funerals of anyone, known or unknown to him, from the community and carrying with him a book of Persian verse in which he took notes as he studied it, sitting on the chairs set out for male mourners while the four days of prayers were said for the departed soul. It really didn't matter to him who had died. A funeral was his haven of peace, away from the clamour of children, away from the accusing eyes of his wife and the other silent womenfolk of the joint-family household who would discuss his guilt shrewishly among themselves but dared not say anything in his presence or hearing.

*

The melancholy of this era of loss has been resident in my grandfather's voice for years, and it cries for recognition as he sings in the bath. He takes me and my sister down the road a few hundred yards for walks to Victoria Gardens, the Bombay Zoo, where we ride the elephants and see the camels, zebras and monkeys. An old man with his memories of grandeur and celebrations in the palaces of maharajas for whom he was a master builder with two and sometimes four children when our male cousins joined us, throwing nuts to the caged monkeys.

I began to know him as the old man whose veins stood out on the back of his brown hand, whose light and life was his first grandchild, my sister. At this age she had light brown hair and a pretty frown.

Bapawaji, as we called him, would sing as he poured water over his head from a bucket in the bathroom, the place whose grilled waterhole was, we imagined, the secret entrance to hell. He would emerge in a towel wrapped around his waist.

I didn't live in Dhondy Terrace. I didn't even live in Bombay. I was brought there now and again from Poona, a town a hundred and twenty miles away by train, inland on the great Deccan plateau, whenever my father, who was in the army and was shunted all over India with a regiment proudly called the Bombay Sappers and Miners, was visiting the ancestral home.

The visiting children, my sister, my cousins and I slept on mattresses on the mosaic floor and in the evenings ate our meals on the balcony.

As we ate our evening meal while the Bombay dusk descended, the singers would pass below, young men with wailing voices, guitars and a determination to relay their tragedies to the world.

"Put another nickel in,
In that Nickelodeon,
And all I want is loving you,
And music, music, music, music"

And the other one who came later, night after night, whose voice was saturated with the disappointments of love:

> *"Irene goodnight Irene,*
> *Irene goodnight,*
> *Goodnight Irene,*
> *Goodnight Irene,*
> *I'll see you in my dreams"*

A lesson in lyric writing. I didn't know what the songs meant, who Irene was, what a nickel or an Odeon was. Music, goodnight and dreams I understood, and like human beings of all ages, I was groping towards understanding "love". Who were these singers? To whom were they singing? Into the other noises of the night they went, into the dark. My grandfather sang:

> *"Aaansoon na baha,*
> *Faryaad na kar,*
> *Dil jalta hai,*
> *Toh jalney dey"*

> Shed no tears,
> Make no complaint,
> If your heart burns
> Let it burn…

I knew it was sad, and it seemed to teach me that all songs were personal and about one's own life because my grandfather's voice as he sang was redolent with confession and the guilt of experience.

And now, so many years later, I am back in Bombay. Its name has changed to Mumbai, and I haven't arrived here as I used to on the four-hour train ride on the Deccan Queen from Poona whose name has now changed to Pune. I arrived on an Air India flight from London where I live. I am here with a friend, a British composer, to compose Hindi songs for a group of Bombay girls sponsored by a Bombay TV station and recording company. In the studio, night after night, Roddy, my co-writer, is trying to work out the melodies on the synthesizer keyboard, and the melancholy of my grandfather's song comes back. Can we use those sad cadences? Can we sentimentalize our girl-group song? I induce Roddy to try. It's perhaps impossible to convey or capture. I sing the song. It's not a trick of melody. It's the genuine product of context, experience. One person's tearjerker is another one's joke.

I tell myself that the emotion must come from the memory, it must be real. I think back and hear the voice. My granddad's voice. The associations of Dhondy Terrace, the terror of the grill through which the water went, the deeper terror of the toilet with the rusty cistern at a height of eight feet and the tall doors that shut behind you as you squatted over the key-shaped ceramic bowl, a toilet so narrow that there was no room for a supervising mother or ayah.

There was an odour of terror, a fragrant ghost in the house; something that had to be locked out, that would creep back from the watery hole of the toilet, seep back through the soapy bubbles at the grill of the bath, or come in through the cracked window in the evening when the music and drumming commenced from the stretch of thatched slum beyond that bathroom window. Maybe it was just my granddad's story, the fall of a generous fool, or the conviction he transmitted after that fall, that there was nothing much more in life than holding the tiny hands of your grandchildren as you walked through the zoo. You didn't look into the abyss, it seeped into the house. Into life.

I don't want that to be true. I want to discover in the cadences of the songs something stolen from the experience of that house, of his song, a dying fall that catches the emotions, that makes the listener cry.

Here I am in a Mumbai studio writing songs with an Englishman. Walking out after a night's work at arrangement and recording, I feel the deserted streets of this district called Lokhandwala, with its impressive new office blocks and still dirty and unpaved footpath, are filled with echoes. Was it Sebastian who in *The Tempest* first heard the sounds of the island?

I want to distil the emotion of the bath-song of my grandfather into a tune, into a cadence that can wring a tear from the hardest heart. The bare emotion of his story must come through. I suggest little trills of tune, but they don't seem to affect Roddy emotionally. I can't tell him what's in my mind. I get him to try out tunes. He says, "Hmm, that's nice. Pretty," as he fingers it out on the keyboard. Of course he doesn't get it. How can he?

Only for me there is heartbreak and disappointment in those tunes. There is the picture of the old man in his light British summer suit, dark circles under his eyes, walking his overdressed grandchildren in Bombay zoo, buying them rides on the mangy elephants. Singing in the bath. I want the tunes to say that. They can't. They won't. Put another nickel in, in that nickelodeon. All I want is loving you and how shall I exploit it? In music, music, music?

⋆

(Added to the First Edition. – fd)

16 Avanbai Mansions
Gorwalla Colony
Mahim,
Mumbai

My Dear Farok,

You may not remember me, but I am your daddy's cousin. Me and my husband follow your columns and other writings and books very diligently but this Deccan Queen book that you have written is a little puzzling because your grandfather never went to funerals to read Persian books. You are mixing him up with my grandfather who was also your father's mother's father and he was called Jamshedji Saklatwalla and he was a real scholar, which I am afraid your grandfather who played polo and all that and drank the best whisky was not. Jamshedji came from a grand aristocratic Parsi landowning family around a village in Gujarat called Saklat and had plenty of cash.

I know this must be a small correction for you and I didn't want to bother you with it but my husband said I must take the opportunity to get in touch with you. Next time you are in Bombay please come and see us and have a meal. We would love to see you.

And by the way, you must know from family folk tales that my grandfather and your great-grandfather, the same Jamshedji, collected manuscripts and paintings. One of the paintings he picked up from a collector in France is supposed to be a missing painting of the painter Titian. It is called *Venus Reclining to Music*. Jamshedji spent a lot of years and a lot of his fortune in travelling in Europe and trying to get the experts to verify and certify that it was actually an original Titian. Unfortunately, though very many of the best galleries, including the Louvre in Paris, were willing to say it was from that period and may have been by one of Titian's students, they were not willing to give it their signature or blessing or whatever you call it. So Jamshedji died without authentically knowing about his painting. This canvas is still with my other cousin as it was passed to my uncle, the eldest son. It is, I am afraid, getting a little bit of fungus in the Mumbai damp weather and needs cleaning up.

Since you are in England and in the world of arts and crafts do you happen to know anybody who would like to see the painting and take matters further? Please tell us.

Your cousins,
Dilshad and Dorab Daruwalla

*

London

Dear Dilshad,

Thanks for your letter. I did know that it was Jamshedji who went to funerals to get away from the clamour of the household, but it didn't suit my fictional purposes to say so.

Allow me to correct an erroneous notion that has obviously circulated in our family for generations.

There is no such place as Saklat in Gujarat—do check with a detailed Survey of India map or nowadays on Google or some other miracle. The family got its name from their trade, which was importing jute from what is now Bangladesh and turning it into cloth for packing for ships' cargoes. Jamshedji's grandfather, father and uncles accumulated their wealth from this trade by selling to the British. Their name Saklatwalla is a corruption of what their British clients called them: Sack cloth walla!

Sorry to dispel illusions about aristocratic wealth, but I for one am much happier with my ancestors carrying on an honest trade, albeit a capitalist one, rather than oppressing and taxing a Gujarati peasantry.

Yes, I shall look into finding an art expert who may be interested in the family Titian.

And of course that Parsi meal in Mumbai when I am next there!

Thanks for getting in touch.

X

Farrukh (correct spelling)

*

London

Dear Dilshad,

Further to our last correspondence, I have a very dear friend Phil who is a qualified curator of fine arts. He has worked at the major museums of Europe and is visiting India with Alberto, his male partner, for a holiday in Goa.

They were not going to stop in Mumbai but I have persuaded him that the *Venus Reclining to Music* belonging to your grandfather and my great-grandfather may be of some interest and perhaps of great value, and he is very curious to have a look. He will stop in Mumbai and bring certain instruments along to carry out some tests. I hope that leads to something. I have given him your phone number, and he will be in touch on getting to Mumbai.

Best wishes,
Farrukh

*

16 Avanbai Mansions
Gorwalla Colony
Mahim,
Mumbai

Dear Farrukh,

First of all let me say sorry for getting the spelling of your name wrong. We were so relieved to get your letter and see that you had not taken offence. Yes you have been very kind in sending Phil over to us and we are eagerly awaiting his visit.

Unfortunately we don't have a very nice flat or even a spare room as our circumstances have changed not for the better so we cannot offer him and Alberto more than a meal or several on their stay in Mumbai. I wish we could say we would put them up, and I feel actually embarrassed at not being able to. I know you and they will understand.

Your loving and grateful cousin,
Dilshad

PS Gratitude for all you are trying for us—this is from Dorab too.

*

16 Avanbai Mansions
Gorwalla Colony
Mahim,
Mumbai

Dear Farrukh,

Whoopee, whoopee, whoopee! Your dear friend Phil, such a gentleman and with his boyfriend who was so amusing, came and visited us, and he took one look at the painting and said, "You definitely have something there. Most certainly, wow! I think I can get some very substantial authentications for this work. Obviously I cannot say whether it's from the hand of the master himself but certainly very close, very close."

These, Farrukh, were his exact words. Phil and Alberto came thrice to the house, and they are charming and have invited us to dinner at their grand hotel tonight.

We are so grateful to you, Farrukh.

Let's see.

Your loving cousin,
Dilshad

*

16 Avanbai Mansions
Gorwalla Colony
Mahim,
Mumbai

Dear Farrukh,

Phil and Alberto are back from Goa, and Dorab and I have agreed, because they are your trusted friends, to allow Phil to ship the painting to London for further conclusive tests. He has himself insured the painting for a vast sum and named us, the owners, as beneficiaries in case anything should happen to the work. We have the insurance certificate, but of course nothing will happen. These eventualities are all melodrama I told Dorab, and what are we going to do with it here. It has been with us for more than a hundred and forty years.

And what shall we do, wait till it crumbles or make some good Parsi pickle out of it?

Phil will get in touch with you as soon as they touch London, and now you will get to see the painting yourself.

Farrukh dear, if this changes our fortunes through your assistance we will not forget you and your kindness, and please believe there are cousins and second cousins of the Saklatwala and the Dhondy clans who need a hand up at this stage in their lives, and we will certainly keep in mind to look after them too.

May the blessings of Ahura Mazda be upon you and your wonderful friends.

Your cuz,
Dilshad

(In college, your father would have told you if he were alive, they used to call me Dildo)

PS Phil said he will only take seven per cent when we have a deal in hand.

*

33a Coleherne Road
London SE 17 PN6

Dear Dilshad and Dorab,

Greetings from rainy London. The painting arrived the day before yesterday, and we have already shown it to two auction houses and to a very rich collector with a private gallery. Of course they say the tests that they will conduct on the paintings will cost approximately £7000 and the cleaning up of the painting without even thinking of any move to restoration will cost a further £11,000.

That's the bad news. The good news is that Jonathan De Burgh, the top expert on Titian from the British Museum, nearly fainted when we called him in this morning. Hold your breath: he thinks this is, if not the real thing, a contemporary facsimile of the third Venus of Titian's trilogy, and of course he was cautious but said it's undoubtedly worth a substantial amount.

We are hiring a security firm to keep watch over it and will bear the costs of that ourselves but must appeal to you to raise the money for the tests and the cleaning up from some source in India or from a joint effort by the potential beneficiaries of this massive bonanza. Sure you can do it. We would help if we could but you know I am a struggling curator and Alberto, despite being a great chef, has no employment right now.

So tell us the next move—we are getting so close.

Your new friends,
Phil and Alberto

*

16 Avanbai Mansions
Gorwalla Colony
Mahim,
Mumbai

Dear Phil,

We are overjoyed at the prospects and really appreciate everything you are doing. We understand the difficulties and are in conversation with a bank now to lend us the money holding our humble flat as security.

You were in and out of here and must have noticed that the flat is nothing much with three rooms and a kitchen and a balcony, but you may have also noticed that it is in a Parsi colony in Mahim, and that makes it very central and very protected and part of prime real estate in Mumbai or Bombay as I still like to call it.

The bank manager seems very positive, and we will let you know. It is almost certain that we will get the loan, and we will discuss at the same time how to get our bank to send it to you.

We are very excited and thank you again for your efforts.

Your good friends,
Dilshad and Dorab

*

33a Coleherne Road
London SE 17 PN6

Dear Dilshad and Dorab,

The expert we talked about, Jonathan De Burgh, brought in two of his colleagues who are very very positive about the possible results of the tests. Of course these can be done without any cleaning or restoration, but the selling price as between us and Jonathan even will be reduced by ten times the cost of cleaning if we don't present, as it were, a perfect picture. Of course that's up to you and the loan you can raise on your flat.

I know you said that you can't do e-mails and don't have a computer and that working with anyone else would mean having to trust them with confidential information and going to a public computer would be risky, but we do think it would speed up communication if you invested in a cheap computer and learnt how to use e-mail.

If you do, our address is Phillalatio@gmail.com

Hoping to hear soonest.
Phil and Alberto

*

From: dilanddo@rediff.com

Dear Phil and Alberto,

See we can do it. We bought a computer, and Mr Irani from next door set it up for us and taught me how to use e-mail. Easy peasy! Now the money can be transferred to your bank as soon as my bank gets government permissions to ship it out. We don't understand these regulations, but our manager at the Central Bank is an old friend and has promised to sort it out as soon as possible.

So we are in full communication now. Hurray!

Your anxious friends,
Dil and Do

*

From: Phillalatio@gmail.com

It's done. It cannot be authenticated as a Titian but is certainly by the hand of one of his disciples and there are strokes which are attributable to the master. The valuation progresses. It will not disappoint. I'll keep it at that for now.

*

16 Avanbai Mansions
Gorwalla Colony
Mahim,
Mumbai

Dear Farrukh,

Sorry to bother you with this but can you please ask your friend Phil to reply to our last few e-mails as I am not sure they are getting through. He also sent us a phone number which we can't get him on as it asks us always to leave a message. We are sure that he is not getting these messages as perhaps we are making a mistake in sending the e-mails and might even have taken the wrong phone number. Just give him a nudge if possible.

And please send us your e-mail too as we are now communicating with everyone through e-mail. So much more convenient and faster. Mind you I still enjoy writing and getting letters! Our e-mail is dilanddo@rediff.com

Thank you in advance.

Your cousins,
Dil and Do

*

From: prisonerofpoona@gmail.com

Dear Dilshad,

Tried to call Phil and Alberto and e-mailed them several times. They must be out of town and not accessing e-mail. I shall, even tomorrow, go over to their place and as you say give them a nudge.

Fd

*

From: prisonerofpoona@gmail.com

Dear Dilshad

Tell me by return of e-mail what you've given Phil and Alberto. I hope the painting is still with you.

Fd

*

From: dilanddo@rediff.com

Dear Farrukh,

I don't know what to make of your last mail. The painting is in London with Phil who has security guarding it. We sent him a bank draft of £15000 to defray expenses. We are now very anxious. Please inform.

Dilshad

*

From: prisonerofpoona@gmail.com

I don't know how to tell you this, but Phil and Alberto are no longer at their address. The flat they rented has been abandoned, and they have done a moonlight flit. I have some leads and will enquire further,

Fd

*

From: dilanddo@rediff.com

Farrukh, the person who will know exactly where the painting is and where your friends are is an art expert from the British Museum called Jonathan De Burgh who was handling the tests, etc. Once you locate them we can get back on course. It is possible that he will know where the painting is being cleaned and precisely dated.

*

From: prisonerofpoona@gmail.com

Dilshad and Dorab,

This is not good news. I made very detailed enquiries—I went three times myself—there is no such person as Jonathan De Burgh. The British Museum people have never heard the name nor do they know the man I knew as Phillip Dobson. He even gave another name to the landlord from whom they rented the flat, calling himself Stephen Fairchild. I will follow up these leads, but don't hold your breath.

*

From: prisonerofpoona@gmail.com

Dilshad,

I went to the police and yesterday they informed me that Phil and Alberto left the country by Argentine Airlines two weeks ago. They took the painting with them as they took out a hefty insurance package on it—no doubt with your money. The police say they will be in touch with Interpol, but the only prospect of tracing these bastards is if they try and sell the work to a museum.

I acknowledge my part in introducing Phil to you and really don't know what I can do to make amends. I have no savings but since *Deccan Queen*'s first edition sold out, the publishers are being persuaded to pay me an advance on a second edition, which they want expanded to include the reactions from the real people featured in the first edition—such as your letters and this correspondence.

I have already informed my agent that the entire advance and any money that the book earns in royalties should be sent directly to you if you will send me your bank details. It may help you in some small way to pay back the loan you took.

Again, I can't tell you how sorry I am.

Yours ever,
Farrukh

The Fall

When anyone left for Bombay, the *tanga* would call at some unholy hour of the morning and take them and their luggage to Poona railway station to catch the Deccan Queen, the fast morning train that would wind its way in less than four hours down the Western Ghats, the highlands that run down the entire western edge of peninsular India and overlook the narrow coastal strip.

I had taken the train with my parents or aunts for as long as I could remember. The early morning wake-up call, the quick hot bath and the suitcases with a change of clothes for the four or five days we were to spend in the Big City before returning to quiet Poona. The bustle of Bombay was even then associated in my mind with danger. But not with sex. I knew nothing about sex then.

I was eight and in school in Poona when I had my first few shamefaced lessons in this dimension of existence from the boys in my class. On my first day at the new school, a lanky, dark-skinned, brazen boy called Udai Laad nudged me and asked if I knew the meaning of "fuck". I did not. He was overjoyed at my admission of ignorance. He told the others in our line-up to the daily religious assembly. Then he asked me if I'd like to know, and I said yes.

He kept me in suspense for a few days. Other boys would come up and ask if I really didn't know the meaning of the word, and I'd have to say I didn't but was willing to find out. They would screech with delight. I was the youngest in the class. The rest were at least one or two years older than I was.

There was a sort of caste division in our school between day scholars and boarders. The boys, like myself, who came and went from home every day were looked upon as uninitiated. The boarders, a great number of them from Bombay, who lived in the miserable dormitories of the school and were paraded to breakfast, lunch, dinner, games, baths, homework sessions and everything else, were treated as the sons of the soil, the hardened elite corps.

Udai was a day scholar like me, and one day in the break he decided that he would put me out of my misery and amuse himself with my initiation into the secret. He made me stick the forefinger of my right hand out, erect, and made a ring of the thumb and forefinger of my left hand. He then brought my two hands together in a simulation of penetrative sex.

"You're doing it now," he said, and some others around us squealed in knowing, boyish delight.

"That's all it is?" I asked.

More squeals. He then proceeded to graphically tell me that what I was doing was a model of the real act, which was done with a penis and a girl's gash in the groin, the place they pissed from.

It was incredible, but self-evidently true. I remember how the absolute truth of it hit me. He had triggered an awareness that was dormant in my blood. Of course that's what one did. I didn't know why, and I didn't even know that girls had special cavities just there, but there was no escape, no side-stepping the fall from grace, the knowledge, if not the foretaste, of the forbidden fruit of Eden. And I felt the fall, the ticklish feeling in the abdomen that accompanies weightlessness. It was a guilty discovery, veiled knowledge that I dare not expose to my sister, my aunts, my mother.

Soon after, one morning, my mother left for Bombay. I asked her why she was going and she gave me a teasing answer. She said it was a secret, but she'd bring me a present when she returned in a week or a fortnight. My father was away in South India on an army "transfer".

The secret bothered me. All the other secrets—what was in the wrapped-up parcel I had to wait for my actual birthday to open, where the whisky was kept to hide it away from the marauding cook, etc.—had been banished from my mind by this big one. While my mother was away I was instructed to bear her absence like a man and to demonstrate no signs of sentimental weakness. If I was sad, it was not something other people wanted to know, and missing Mum was not what grown-up boys did.

On one of those days, when I couldn't stop the panic in my chest about my mum's absence, a spread of photographs from a news magazine began to circulate around my class. They passed the magazine's photographs from a cluster of boys around one desk to a scurry of boys around the next. The magazine feature was about the "cages" of Bombay and portrayed dark-skinned naked women from the red-light district of the city, their eyes masked out with black strips to protect their shameless identities.

Very few of the boys knew precisely what they were looking at. A Bombay lad, a boarder at the school, more knowing than the rest, explained in bursts what the trade of prostitution was about. The women took money for doing it. They came from everywhere in India to Bombay, and to Foras Road especially, to enter these cages and make money. It was a secret trade.

It was the most shameful or shameless thing I had ever heard, and a terror gripped my insides. I couldn't allow the pictures and associations that began to suggest themselves to even swim out of the depths of my contaminated mind. The thoughts must be suppressed as a dull, explosive ache. And never seeing the light they would remain dark, shadowy, accusing.

As I lay in bed that night, they came to the surface like piranha fish. Why had she gone to Bombay? Over dinner that evening I had approached the subject.

"Why has mummy gone to Bombay?" I asked my aunt.

"She has some business there," she said off-handedly.

"What business?" I asked.

"Why does it bother you? She's got to get some money from some gentlemen. She said she'd get you a present. You're going to be rich."

"Where is she living?"

"What's the matter, she has twenty places to live," my aunt said, urging me to eat up the spinach she had dished onto my plate.

I thought she was fending the questions off. What money was Mum getting? Doesn't daddy give her money? I didn't sleep well that night.

My mother returned from Bombay bearing tainted gifts.

Bombay began to occupy the territory of my imagination associated with shame, with deceit, with the fall of Eve.

*

I never asked where the money for the gifts she had brought from Bombay came from. I was terrified of the possible answer. I tried to put the episode out of my mind, but its terror lingered. Then the time came to visit Bombay myself.

From the age of eight onwards, I regularly went during the school holidays with my boy cousins to Bombay, a city from which everything emanated—the fads and the finery. Until that time I looked forward to going and spending time with my Bombay cousins and walking the pavements on which these gee-gaws were reputedly on sale.

Self-consciousness about clothes and fashions was just setting in. We were beginning to treat the visit to the barber as an exercise in shaping one's looks instead of what it used to be—the compulsory and periodic descent into the torture chamber.

At the time, amongst us pre-pubescents in Poona, there was a brisk trade in cheaper gee-gaws than those available on the streets or perhaps even the school playgrounds of Bombay. We traded in marbles and tops and y-shaped bits of branch from which catapults could be constructed with rubber bands cut from old bicycle tubes and a leather piece known as a *piddi* to hold the projectile. Boys with high profiles, the "characters" of the school, would acquire unusual little bits of leather and put them up for auction. One particular piddi, very lightly coloured and thick, was auctioned for a phenomenal number of marbles because its owner claimed that it was a "camel's balls' piddi", a fragment of a camel's scrotum. There were other fabulous piddis in circulation. A prized one was a tiger-skin piddi, and it was said that the genuine article would last a lifetime. None of us envisaged that a time would come when we might put away catapults and move on.

Vanity and bad taste slowly began to replace this boyish utilitarian hankering. Bombay invaded Poona with trinkets and adornments bought on the pavements of the big city. Boys in the school began wearing jewellery—metal rings with "Red Indian" heads carved on them, metal crosses on chains, bracelets with one's name engraved on silver plates, thick leather belts with very special metal buckles and the like. The large rings were rare and treasured as it was said they could be used as knuckle dusters in self-defence and were reputed to be able to crack an opponent's jaw open on contact.

And now I was, as the routine of the year dictated, back with my cousins in Bombay.

My cousins' parents lived on the fringe of the southern bay of Bombay, a smart waterfront called Marine Drive. My cousins were tough guys, turning up their short sleeves to show their biceps, and in the holidays had enrolled in the sea scouts, drawing on family tradition, as their father was a senior officer in the Indian Navy. While they were away a few days a week at sea scout training sessions, I remained alone in their ocean-side flat, read books, played with the dog or wandered out in the ceaseless quest for a Red Indian ring and a Red Indian belt buckle on which I'd set my heart. They were nowhere to be found. Bombay, the city of everything, disappointed.

The house was not far from the Eros cinema opposite Churchgate railway station, the terminus of the local railway system that ran vertically up the length of the island and brought thousands of commuters into the commercial and official districts each morning. One afternoon, my uncle and aunt left the three of us, my cousins and myself, at the cinema to see a film called *The Wings of the Hawk*. It must have been a "cowboy" movie, but I can't remember its content. For a reason. Was I nine, or ten?

As we watched the film the hand of the stranger sitting next to me strayed to my hand. The contact, I thought, was obviously chance and innocent. I withdrew my hand to my side by degrees, but his hand, again seemingly in complete relaxation, followed mine and insisted on brushing against it. I withdrew my hand to my lap. Which was precisely what he must have wanted me to do, because he casually moved his hand across to mine and began to stroke it as though he was resuming a connection we had unwittingly lost.

The stroking may have been physically pleasant from a parent or a family elder, a deliberate and gentle token of affection, but this, from a stranger, was mixed with embarrassment and apprehension. It was on the one hand a definite gesture, not a mistake any more, but on the other, much too vague to make an embarrassing protest about.

The hand acquired confidence by my silence and frozen inaction. It went to my leg, clad in shorts, and began working its way up my thigh. I looked in consternation at the man. He was staring straight at the screen as though his hand had an autonomous will and was behaving in this outrageous way of its own accord. I tried to push the hand away, but it became forcefully stubborn now, the fingers feeling their way towards my crotch, which was shrinking at the touch.

The orchestral score of *The Wings of the Hawk* came to a climax and the lights came on. It was the interval. The hand was withdrawn. The man leant over to me as though we were friends and asked if he could buy me an ice cream or some such. I said no, and he left smiling, saying I was to keep his place for him. He was a young fresh-faced man and spoke English after the fashion of the city.

My elder cousin asked me what the man had said to me, and I told him that the fellow was trying to push his hand into my trousers. I said I wanted to go, I was frightened. My cousin said I would have to stay, because he wanted to see the rest of the film, but he volunteered to take care of it and said I was to change places with him. He then went off to the toilets.

I took his seat and sat tight. The man came back, and when he found I had moved a seat, asked me quite brazenly why I had done that. I said my cousin wanted to sit on that side. He was undeterred.

"Shall I sit between the two of you? Two lovers?" he said and laughed. "We could all have a good time playing."

I didn't know how to respond.

"I think my cousin wants to sit there," I said.

"Is he a friendly fellow? Like you?" the man asked.

Before I could reply my cousin was back and gave the man an unfriendly scowl.

The lights faded, and the film started as we settled down. Relief flooded through my body. Was it tinged with the slightest regret? Had I turned back from a forbidden adventure that would have remained a secret between this stranger and me, through cowardice? My body knew that beyond the stroke on the thigh there was a promise of some further arousal, a pleasure that still lay dormant in my pre-pubescent flesh.

As *The Wings of the Hawk* spread themselves on the screen, I dared not look to my left to see how the man was progressing with my cousin. I heard the fellow whispering to my cousin, "Can I play with your little man?"

"Bugger off!" my cousin said, loud enough for the whole cinema to hear. It was his best simulation of an adult growl. The man didn't wait for enquiry and the public retribution that might have followed if the accusation of molestation was picked up by the audience next to and behind us. He stood up and hastily made his way down the row and out of the cinema, covering his face with one hand.

I watched him go, my stomach knotted. He was no innocent lover, not one who had fallen into a chance encounter; his panic and flight made him what I knew even as a child was a child-molester stalking the cinemas looking for game, for *shikar*. Would he be waiting for us in the shadows as we went home?

*

(Miriam, my aunts didn't live to see Deccan Queen published but I remember talking to them about the time I "lost my innocence" as they would have put it, and the time Mum went to Bombay on her secret business. It seems she had inherited some shares from a distant relative who had died and left the original or founders' shares in the Hong Kong and Shanghai bank to the family. Mum had gone to the Bombay solicitors to claim the family's surprise inheritance, and it was supposed to be confidential till all the verifications of identity, etc., were complete. Not a very exciting "secret" but that's what it was. Perhaps the mundane revelation ought to go into the Second Edition. – fd)

An Indian Passage

Bayview
Mount Mary Avenue
Bandra,
Bombay,
India

2 January 1931

Dear Mama and Papa,

From where I write I can look out over the choppy Arabian Sea right to the clear horizon where gulls swoop down and fly towards the rocks on the shore below us where they nest, I presume. I can see a steamer out at sea and fancy that one of those will be carrying this letter to you as soon as I finish it and send the maid (she is a papist, speaks English haltingly and is called Immaculata, if you please!) to post it.

Christmas in Bombay is delightful and delightfully warm. No rain, no snowflakes and no bitter wind. One hears through the telegraph that England has had deep snow. I hope Saffy is blanketed and kept warm, and maybe shut the cat-flap so she doesn't get cat-flu from the snow?

The Romans celebrate their Christmas with candles, and they carol their way up the hill just before our bungalow. The Carruthers set up a little nest atop the wall by the gate from which we could view the procession, all carrying candles. Mr Charles Carruthers tells me that their papist church was established here by the Portuguese long before we set foot on these islands, but it was we who cleared it (the island, not the church!) of swamp and malaria once we had acquired it from the Portuguese as part of the dowry of Charles II, the Portuguese being too indolent to have bothered.

This church to the Mother of God stands a furlong atop the hill, and the procession winds its way there, led by their priests, and one may hear their prayers as the silence descends on the hill.

For New Year we went down into the City of Bombay by the harbour where there is a garrison and the young officers throw a ball each year.

I have a letter from Aunt Vicky who says she and the Colonel are looking forward to my visit to Poona next week. She is very kind and very discreet, and though she knows you have talked about everything she only writes that she longs to introduce me to her young friends. She mentions two couples, a Captain and Mrs Sissons and a Major and Mrs Tombs! The Major will accompany four of us ladies, as our guide and protector, to the interior, as he happens to be in Bombay. No mention of dashing Mr Foggerty.

Ah well!

I've been reading a perfectly beastly book by a Mr E.M. Forster about a young woman coming out to India to be betrothed. Most unengaging so far.

Please, please write back soon.

Your very loving,
Corinthia

*

33 Stanley Road
Poona Cantt.
India

8 Jan. 1931

My dear Mama and Papa,

The train ride from Bombay to Poona is the most delightful of journeys a creature can undertake! It's a dream. One goes inland from the coast, and the steam from the engine wafts past the window, which has intriguing wooden shutters.

We stop at a place called Cur-jot and are allowed to alight and inspect the engine and talk to the engineer who is a Mr Cumberbatch from Cornwall. The rake, which sweeps dead cattle and other country debris in front of it, is coloured a bright red.

Mr Cumberbatch threw in the "dead cattle" with a twinkle in his eye, and I caught his glance and surmised that he was only saying it to tease the ladies.

He tells us that another engine driver whom he refers to quite endearingly as his "partner", a

Mr Holloway, will drive another engine from the top of the mountains, which he refers to as "Goths". He explains that there is only a donkey track up the looming mountains, and the railway, which is even now being carved out through them, will take a further year to complete.

We can see the mountains, but I remark that they don't seem to loom. Mr Cumberbatch frowns. He wants his mountains to loom.

Miss Cole, whom I have befriended on the journey, is quite indignant and protests that she will under no circumstances ride a donkey up the mountain, and Major Tombs has to intervene to say that Mr Cumberbatch, with whose wry humour he is familiar, was saying it in jest. We are to take a very narrowly built coach pulled by a string of horses.

We bid adieu to Mr C with his blue jacket and red scarf and coal-scarred face and take this coach.

The rest of the journey is even more eventful, but I shall save it for the next letter because I must tell you that Aunt Vicky lost no time in inviting Mr Foggerty to tea. What can I say? He looks nothing like the photographs that Uncle Eb sent us. He is much more substantial, a person of girth, and age has scarred his jowls. He says very little so I cannot yet tell if he is agreeable in other ways.

Your loving daughter,
Corinthia

*

33 Stanley Road
Poona Cantt.
India

14 March 1931

My dearest Mama and Papa,

Your letter made me homesick, but I got over it through the distractions of the vigorous existence we lead here. Uncle Eb goes riding at five-thirty in the morning every day and Aunt Vicky and I join him on Saturdays. The evenings are given to the Gymkhana, which is a club where one may play cards or croquet and where the men haunt the bars.

Poona is lovely. You ask about Mr Foggerty. He is rather keen and has asked me out to dinner at the same Italian restaurant, called Muratto's, twice. His conversation is all about trade and rather dull though he will not say quite what he does. He says he is a very "big cheez" in the Eastern Tobacco Company, but won't say whether he grows it or sells it or only smokes it. By the way, in case you've ever wondered, I was told, though not by Mr F, that a "big cheez" is not a fromage, but that the Urdu word for a "thing" is "cheez" from which we get big cheez meaning grand personage! So there! (actually Mr Cumberbatch, the train engineer, who happened to be travelling back from Poona on the Deccan Queen when Uncle Eb and I went down to Bombay for the yacht races, told me that. He was on a busman's holiday he said.

He didn't have his red scarf and jacket and was, as gentlemen do here, wearing a cotton suit and cravat.

Uncle Eb wasn't that keen when he stopped by and recognized me and I, him, despite the lack of uniform! I am sure Aunt Vicky will write and complain that I have taken to indulging the servants in conversation, but trust me, all I have done is transgressed the laws of Anglo-Indian snobbery of which there is a lot! Oh, and Mr Foggerty was racing a yacht, and it was at his invitation that Uncle Eb and I went down to Bombay, and he was very disconcerted when Mr Cumberbatch, an off-duty engineer, presumed to stop and converse. All he could say was "The likes of him shouldn't be given First Class passes!")

The first leg of the journey by the Deccan Queen takes one from Poona station to a place called Lone-valla and thence to a smaller outpost called Kand-valla. The train goes along a ridge on the mountaintops and stops. One has a magnificent view of the valleys below and on a clear day the coastal strip of western India. Here one alights. The ridge is known to the cognoscenti as "the reversing" (again, a snippet I picked up from the indefatigable Mr Cumberbatch) as the train turns back from there to return to Poona with its load of passengers who have been hauled up the "Goths" by donkeys. I discovered my error—the narrow coach was not drawn by horses but by mules. How undignified! But one is told that they are safer on mountains because of the donkey content in their blood.

Am still reading this ghastly novel by Mr Forster, which has a lady who comes to India finding herself mesmerized by some native doctor. The only natives I have encountered in four months here are the servants! Native doctors indeed! I mention it because Uncle Eb asked me what I was reading while we were on the train, and I had to prevaricate and put it by.

As one rides down the mountains to the coastal plain through several cuttings and tunnels winding this way and that, tribes of monkeys clamber over the coaches and chatter and beg for food and grimace menacingly. One has to keep the windows tightly shut.

There are plunging narrow waterfalls that sometimes appear suddenly as the mule-train rounds a corner of a rock cliff. A lot of green shrubbery covers the Goths.

The yacht races from the tip of Bombay out into the ocean, which is called the Arabian Sea, were very exciting to watch except that "our" boat with Mr Foggerty and his Eastern Tobacco team nearly capsized at the start and then went on to come last.

Your loving daughter,
Corinthia

*

33 Stanley Road
Poona Cantt.
India

20 June 1931

Dear Mama and Papa,

The Monsoons have "broken" as they say, and I feel the expression attempts a description of the sky being breached and the waters of some heavenly ocean pouring down and soaking the earth. It really is a deluge, not so much in Poona but much more so when we risked the trip as Aunt Vicky said, and came foolishly down to Bombay because Uncle Eb has a share in a racehorse that died, and the partners, being business people in Bombay, refused to return his share. It has led to some form of legal wrangling, but the upshot was that we had to come to the courts in the city.

We started from Poona by the Deccan Queen, and it happened that the same Mr C of whom I have spoken encountered us on the platform as he was making his way to the engine to drive it. Another train with windowless carriages all the colour of dull brick passed through the station and gave off a very powerful smell of stinking fish. Mr C told us, as we held our noses and voiced our revulsion, that this was known as the "Bombay Dak", the mail train from Bombay, and it was indeed packed with dried fish from the coast, which were now being shipped by the ton to the interior as they've become part of the staple native diet. Uncle Eb didn't seem impressed but I noted, very loudly for the company to hear, that Mr C was full of such delightful pointers on the foibles of this continent.

It poured with rain as the train pulled out, and the clouds got thicker and were rolling like a galloping herd of cattle as we reached the mountains at the edge of the plateau from whence we were supposed to descend by mule train.

It was not to be. The mountain road, they told us as they turned us back on the train, had been swept away by the rain, and the mules were not sure-footed enough to cross the swept debris, however urgent our missions in Bombay might be.

We returned to Poona and were met at the station by Mr Foggerty in his motor.

Uncle Eb wrote several letters to his co-owners, and on getting no reply decided it was no use flogging a dead horse—his little joke—and decided to set aside his claim.

Aunt Vicky found the book by Mr Forster that I was reading by my bedside and confiscated it. She said the whole of India, by which she meant Europeans, knew about it, and it was a wicked calumny on the Anglo-Indian community and was unsuitable reading for a young lady. She thought it ought not to be on sale in this or any other country as she said foreigners and Indians may take heart from the misinformation and bigotry therein. As a consequence I have no idea whether the native doctor was hanged for his crimes or not. Very annoying, but you know how unbending Aunt Vicky is.

Your loving daughter,
Corinthia

*

Bayview
Mount Mary Avenue
Bandra,
Bombay,
India

29 June

Dear Papa,

I know the ship hasn't come in so don't expect any mail from England for the next fortnight. But I so look forward to your letters—or shall I say Mother's letters signed by you.

Now, Papa, I am sending this to you at your office address because I want to take you into my confidence and keep these matters from Mama till I receive your advice, which I will, I promise, diligently and unquestioningly follow.

I am in a muddle, dear Pater. I am only clear on the fact that Aunt Vicky will have conveyed her side of what I consider a sorry tale to Mama. She and Mama think that I want to thwart their plans.

The truth is, Papa, I find Mr Foggerty, whom they seem to have chosen for me, not to my taste. To put no finer a point on it, he is disgusting in appearance, being somewhat obese, with red circles under his eyes and hair cascading from his ears and nose. The photographs Aunt Vicky and he have contrived to send to Mama are quite deceptive. His conversation is limited to talk of trade and of shipping news and forecasts, matters in which I have no interest. I mentioned to him the book that was confiscated by Aunt Vicky, the novel by Mr Forster, and he seemed quite bewildered by the fact that anyone had dared to write a fictionalized account of a romance about India.

He has no opinions on books or literature and tirelessly reads the trade gazettes. I mentioned in passing a book by Mr Henry James that I adore, and he said he wouldn't read anything by an American and then extended the opinion that King George III was not sufficiently forceful and allowed the colony to lapse to the colonials whom he characterized as the "riff-raff of Europe".

Uncle Eb is, as I expect his position as a magistrate requires, very engaged with the politics of India and full of opinions at tea about the doings of their Mr Gandy and Mr Nero and the rest, and he attempted on several occasions to elicit an opinion on these subjects from Mr Foggerty who merely grunted and virtually opined that Uncle Eb and his fellows on the bench were too lenient with mischievous demagogues.

He wears a brown suit and brown shoes, Papa.

I have attempted to express my inability to engage with Mr Foggerty, but Aunt Vicky's response amounted to the implication that I was conceited and could do no better than he. I know that Uncle Eb knows I spent the next day in my room and in the garden in a state of despair. I own that I cried, Papa, that Aunt Vicky, who has only known me as an infant and these last few months, should think so little of me. I know I am no beauty but hope to make up for it through what kindness and generosity I am capable of.

What transpired three days ago was most disagreeable. You will have noted that I have mentioned a certain engine driver, a Mr Cumberbatch from Cornwall, a personage who, considering his profession, is very knowledgeable and even on our last encounter told me that Mr Forster's novel didn't end with the hanging of the native doctor but with an Englishman befriending him in a possibly questionable relationship on which he, Mr Cumberbatch, could not elaborate to a lady.

Three days ago I was reading in the garden when I heard an altercation between the chowkidar, a sort of sentry or gatekeeper, and an English voice. I ventured to the gate to investigate the matter and to my pleasant surprise found Mr Cumberbatch seeking entrance to the house.

I asked him, naturally, what brought him here, and he said he had in my presence on the train spoken to my Uncle Eb and would like to talk to him on a certain matter. I happened to know that Uncle Eb was not at home at that moment but was expected back for tea so I invited Mr Cumberbatch to accompany me into the house.

Being thus escorted, no further fuss was made by the chowkidar, and I invited Mr Cumberbatch into the sitting room, whereupon he took his seat with his hat in his lap, a trifle awkwardly, while I went to invite Aunt Vicky to meet him as he awaited Uncle Eb's arrival.

To my utter consternation and disgrace, Aunt Vicky swept into the sitting room and without waiting for my introduction to him or my explanation as to Mr Cumberbatch's presence, she asked him to leave.

"He has business with Uncle Eb whom he spoke to when we met on the Bombay train, Aunt Vicky. You were there," I protested.

"My memory is very clear. It wasn't an encounter we sought. And your uncle's good breeding doesn't certify its beneficiaries. Now, sir, please leave my house," she said.

Mr Cumberbatch didn't hesitate, but darted to the door.

"My regards to the Magistrate-Sahib," he said.

"I invited him, Aunt Vicky!" I shouted.

"You should not have. You don't live in India and wouldn't understand the necessary discretion," she said.

I ran after Mr Cumberbatch, even though Aunt Vicky tried sternly to stop me. I caught him up fifty yards down the road outside the gate.

"I am so sorry. It was my fault, my misjudgement," I said.

"I wasn't not expecting to be told to be off, if you get my drift," he said and smiled, and then, uncannily, "You don't live in India and wouldn't understand the necessary discretion."

He certainly couldn't have overheard her words and repeated them ironically. He meant them—in his own way.

"But Mr Cumberbatch, what can I do to remedy the awful position I put you in and the insult you suffered?"

"You can do two things," he said. "You can call me Eric and you can meet me on Saturday afternoon at Wellington Hotel tea-rooms as my guest. It's when I am next in town. By then I expect the case will be over and the poor beggars jailed."

My frown was my question but he didn't want to elaborate.

"I must get on," he said. "And you are in enough trouble already. I don't expect you to speak on my behalf. Good afternoon, Miss Corinthia."

He must have seen and memorized my name from the reservation list of the Deccan Queen.

The poor beggars of whom he spoke were two native railway employees who worked under Mr Cumberbatch and who had been apprehended stealing cages full of live young chickens from the goods train going from the interior to Bombay. They had been taken away in handcuffs and with ropes around their necks to be detained and tried, and Mr Cumberbatch was, said Uncle Eb when we discussed the matter, probably seeking a meeting with him to intercede in the process of justice on their behalf.

"An approach of that sort is inappropriate," Uncle Eb said and, I suspect not quite meaning it, "He would have been in trouble so I am glad your Aunt Vicky saw him off!"

Aunt Vicky, smarting from my disobedience in running after Mr C, didn't speak to me for two days.

Mr Foggerty called, and I in turn refused to see him. She was infuriated and has already sent off a missive to Mama, as no doubt you will hear, with an invitation to judge my impetuousness.

I judged it best not to accept Mr Cumberbatch's Saturday invitation to tea at the hotel and sent a note to that effect to await him at the reception desk. I apologized profusely and asked him to understand my position. It was, to say the least, an uncomfortable one, and at least one other in the household gauged my suffering. With Uncle Eb's assistance I made an excuse to get to Bombay. The Carruther's third grandchild was being christened so there was occasion enough to make the short break.

Well, Papa, I was accompanied by Uncle Eb to the railway station early last morning to catch the Deccan Queen. As I expected, Mr Cumberbatch was in his working uniform and came strolling down the platform when he saw us. Quite by chance Uncle Eb spotted Mr Foggerty at the same time and called out to him. I turned to look and saw him supervising a retinue of half-naked natives who were carrying large crates on trolleys to the further platform.

Mr Foggerty came over, huffing and puffing, and greeted us whereupon Mr Cumberbatch withdrew and got on, I presumed, with his business of getting the train moving. Which he did. And as it moved off, I waved to Uncle Eb and saw Mr Foggerty rushing after his porters posthaste.

At the reversing, where we change from the train to the mule carriages, Mr Cumberbatch found me.

"I am profoundly sorry about the tea," I said.

"And there I was with my hair cut and my Sunday best on Saturday," he said laughing. "But I had the feeling that you might stand me up."

"That wasn't the intention at all. I was under severe duress as I explained," I said.

"Don't!" he said, holding out a forbidding palm. "That handsome young man—a family friend?"

"Oh Mr Foggerty? A favourite of the aunt you encountered but no more than that."

"She turns away engine drivers but is quite comfortable then with undertakers," he said.

"He works in Eastern Tobacco, a very respectable firm," I said.

"Well, he's constantly shipping dead bodies from the interior to Bombay port," he said.

"I don't understand," I said.

"Those crates the coolies were wheeling, that's what they were—corpses in chemical to preserve them over the voyage to Europe. Hundreds of corpses, shipped out."

"Who? I mean what for? Whose corpses? Mr Cumberbatch … Eric … you are not making sense."

He grinned and said, "Your friend is Poona's collector of corpses. Thousands of people come into the city and die on the pavements—hunger, disease, despair. You've seen it, Miss Corinthia, or you've not seen India. And if their bodies are not claimed, the police have them cremated or sell them to your Mr Foggerty who exports them to Blighty and France and Germany and Sweden where they are needed by universities and medical colleges for experiments and the study of anatomy. All human bodies, saving size and sex, are the same, you know."

I didn't know.

"That's what your man, Mr Foggerty, the one marked out for you by your aunt, does for a living. It's honest enough," he said.

"What do you know about my aunt and her markings," I said. I was stung by his impertinence and the cocky way he said this.

"I know quite a lot about it, Miss Corinthia," he said. "This body salesman is your intended, and you've travelled or been sent a long way from Wiltshire to make the match."

"I don't know what you can mean or how you pretend this intelligence," I said, ready to turn away from him. But I was curious as to how he knew anything about me.

He anticipated the question on my lips.

"I have several days of sojourn in Bombay, Miss Greenford. The best source of all information about society is the Indian servants who work for them." He smiled. "If you will promise not to in any way punish her for divulging her intelligence, I may trust and tell you."

"Immaculata," I said.

"First, the promise?"

"Yes, promise!"

He nodded.

"And you find it perfectly honourable to speak to natives about their employers?"

He began to laugh.

"Miss Greenford, I never expected that from you. Of course I speak to the natives as you call them."

"I think the very idea of spying on someone in that way is an act of low meanness," I said and turned away.

"And yet hearing it from a white man or from some woman at the mahjong table in the Gymkhana would be acceptable, would it?" he shouted after me.

I walked away towards the coaches and he followed me.

"Adela," he shouted.

I turned round. He surely was not calling me Adela. But he was.

"What did you call me, Mr Cumberbatch?"

"I apologize. It slipped out. You occupy my mind a great deal, Miss Corinthia. One's mind is idle while the steam puffs away to the cities of the plains. I have been comparing you to a personage in a book."

"I happen to know the book and find the comparison odious," I said.

"How so?"

"The person can't make up her mind. She doesn't know what she wants or what the truth is."

"Do any of us? India helps her find what she wants. And I have been hoping that it helps you do the same."

I think, Papa, I blushed. I could feel that this young man had intents and purposes which I had not, till that moment, suspected. I dare say this to you as a preface to my further confusion. Papa, I came away from that encounter knowing very firmly that Mr Foggerty was not for me.

I suppose the wretched serving-girl Immaculata must have told Mr Cumberbatch that on dry days I took a walk unaccompanied at six in the evening down the hill towards the beach to watch the sunset. He was waiting for me at the bottom of the hill and confirmed after greeting me that he had been so informed by Immaculata from whom he had sought the intelligence of my routines.

"Is that a decent thing to do? To trust the word of a servant girl? How far will you go, Mr Cumberbatch?"

"As far as I am permitted," he muttered almost inaudibly.

He began to walk by my side down the hill, keeping his distance to the circumference of my wide umbrella.

"You see, I don't see 'natives' and 'servant girls'. Just as I don't see Ladies, Gentlemen and engine drivers."

"More fool you," I said.

"Would you then care to have dinner with me at the Connemara Hotel tomorrow, Corinthia?"

He had dispensed with the niceties of title. I hesitated before replying.

"I am not as impetuous as the young lady in the book, you know. But I am interested in finding out what became of her in the later chapters as the book was taken from me as unsuitable."

"That can certainly be part of the conversation," he replied. "I was going to make it so without being invited to."

"Then may we make it lunch? I don't think dinner would meet with the approval of my hosts who also see themselves as my guardians."

"Ah! I see. So you mean to lie to them about where you shall be going? Sunday. Church perhaps?"

He had read my intent as that was precisely what I had made up my mind to do—to say I would meet a friend and go to church downtown in Colaba. That would give me a few hours away alone.

"Yes, I intended to lie."

"I hope you mean intend," he said.

We had reached the edge of the beach and the sun was setting. It gets to be a beautiful orange orb and grows larger as it descends, beyond the little fishing boats that bob about the bay and come landward, hurrying home before dark, and sinks into the Arabian Sea.

"From the hills at the reversing, on a clear day, and from particular high points on the Ghaats (which is how, in an Indian affectation, he pronounced "the

Goths", the western hills) one can glimpse the sea and the sunset. Even more distant and beautiful."

"I'd like to see that one day."

"I am sure you will," he said and then, "May I accompany you back up the hill towards the house?"

I consented.

"Where are you accommodated ... I mean living?" I asked.

"Oh not too far away, and I suppose the most one can call it is accommodation—railway quarters across the creek."

"To which you'll walk?"

"Oh no," he said, and as we turned from the beach road to the road up the hill, he put two fingers in his mouth and in the manner of a street urchin, let out a piercing whistle, whereupon a tonga, a horse carriage, came trotting our way.

"Dattu has been waiting for me. My own personal carriage. Courtesy of Southern Maratha railways."

The tonga came clomping up to us and Mr C spoke to the native tongawalla. He must have told him to wait.

He did take me to lunch the next day at the Connemara Hotel, which was a complete mistake, Papa, because we were seen lunching there by neighbours of the Carruthers who were informed of my dereliction even before I got back that afternoon.

Sir Charles was waiting for me and was pacing the living room and terrace. I immediately knew that Mrs Carruthers had entrusted the task of confronting me to him. He was as kind as could be. If they could no longer trust me, he said, they could no longer take responsibility for being my guardians. I took it that they wished me to leave and said I had planned to return to Poona the next day. He said that would be fine, and their motorcar drove me to the railway station to take the Deccan Queen the next evening.

I had no way of ascertaining whether Mr Cumberbatch was our engine driver till we got to the bottom of the Goths and had to change. He wasn't and I must say I was, to my own surprise, subject to an emotion I had to own, disappointed.

Papa, I tell you all this because I know you will get their side of these events and my mendacity from Aunt Vicky and Mrs Carruthers.

I beg you not to think badly of me and with your proven ability to get Mama to think that your thoughts and opinions actually germinated in her mind and originated in her generous and rounded character, you will see that Mama doesn't either.

Your loving and only daughter,
Corinthia

*

33 Stanley Road
Poona Cantt.
India

18 July 1931

My dear Mama and Papa,

I have had no reply to my last missive. I hope all is well.

The last few days have been extremely unpleasant. Aunt Vicky, before she left, contrived to see that Mr Foggerty and I were left alone in the garden over tea so he could make his odious proposal to me. It took me quite by surprise when Mr Foggerty produced an engagement ring, presuming, as he had no right to, that I would fall into his arms.

I confess I was not kind and was so startled by this turn of events and in fact suddenly overtaken by an urge to run as far as I could from the scene and his insolent presence, that I must have inadvertently grinned. I admit I thought it absurd and saw myself caught in this charade of absurdity. Mr Foggerty immediately took offence and colouring, asked me in a savage tone what it was that I found amusing. I said I found nothing amusing and fumbled some reply about not being ready to enter any condition of engagement with anybody.

His features turned to a scowl.

"What do you think your aunt and the judge will say when I tell them how you insulted me, eh?"

"I apologize if you thought I insulted you. I never intended to. Or to brush aside your proposal. I am sorry."

"So you want to play hard to get? You are not getting any younger, Miss, and you come, may I say, with no great fortune and no overwhelming beauty," he said, putting his ring back in a little box and tucking it into his waistcoat.

"I am sorry to hear your opinion of my prospects and will now take your leave."

"Damn you," he said, turning red with rage.

I ran into the house and locked my bedroom door. I was shaking.

Aunt Vicky knocked an hour later.

"So, madam, you have turned down the only opportunity you had for shelter from the disgrace you brought upon yourself."

"Aunt Vicky, I despise Mr Foggerty and would rather be burnt at the stake than accept his overtures. And please, I have not committed any sin. I merely went for lunch with a gentleman whose companionship is interesting."

"An engine driver! And if he were not, didn't he encourage you to lie so you could carry on in this fashion with him?"

"What fashion, Aunt Vicky? What have I done?"

"You've lied and cheated to the Carruthers and to us. You have violated the trust that your parents place in us as your guardians by forming an untenable liaison with a serving man. You have turned down the prospect of being the lady of the house of a director of a very respectable commercial house. You forced your uncle and I to resort to concealment. Would he have proposed if he knew the truth of where and with whom you'd gone in Bombay? Would he want a liar for a fiancé?"

That was it, though she said she would consider what to say to you in a letter she was going to write that very night.

This morning I screwed my courage to the sticking place and at breakfast announced to Aunt Vicky and Uncle Eb what I had discovered of Mr Foggerty's business. I told them that he sells corpses for a living, and both of them were incredulous and doubted my word as he had let it be generally known in society that he traded as a factor in a tea and tobacco company and was soon to be its director and live in Calcutta.

Aunt Vicky was more than incredulous. She accused me of severe libel under the influence of people who lived off malice and gossip.

My words echoed in my mind, and a feeling of absurdity overcame me. I found myself sounding like some character out of a Jane Austen romance and determined then to present a more earthy reason for my rejection.

"I couldn't sleep with a man who sells corpses," I said. "And his mouth smells of old socks!"

Uncle Eb left the breakfast table, and Aunt Vicky was aghast at my boldness. There seemed to be nothing more to say.

I am writing this at night. I shall tell Aunt Vicky that I should book my passage home from Bombay as soon as it can be arranged. Aunt Vicky and Uncle Eb have been models of kindness, and it is unfortunate that there can be no agreement on my prospects. I pray that Uncle Eb will out of curiosity at least investigate Mr F's true business and that will vindicate the source of my information. I am positive that when he and Aunt V find out that Mr F has undertaken this gruesome trade on behalf of his company they will support my decision.

I have no doubt that you both, who have given me love and care all my life, would not wish me to form a liaison that would not make me happy. What's more, despite their approval I am sure you would not countenance Mr F as an acquaintance, leave aside as a son-in-law.

Yours anxiously,
Corinthia

*

3E Railway Quarters
Kirkee,
Poona

30 September 1931

My dearest Mama and Papa,

I have also written to Uncle David and asked him to plead with you not to return my letters unread. I hope, with a sinking feeling in my chest, that my last letter was returned through some error of the mails and not because you refused to accept it. I have heard nothing from you since I made my decision and took a step that you probably consider to be unacceptable. I beg you to think of my happiness, which is now only incomplete because I don't have your approval.

I know it seems that I acted impulsively, and I also know that Uncle Eb and Aunt Vicky have my interest at heart, but their apprehensions are misplaced and their judgement terminally distorted by the enclosed world in which they live.

Mother and Father, you don't understand Anglo-India. It is a cauldron of intrigues and lies and self-deceptions with snobberies and social judgements born of what I suppose is the assumption that the environment is hostile.

The Anglo-India of the Carruthers and of Aunt Vicky and Uncle Eb and of the Officer's Mess, the regiment, the district court and the gymkhanas and hotels is a fortress of wrong-minded opinion. It shuts out the ordinary serving soldier and even the British men and women who come or are sent here to serve the Empire as workers—and yes I do mean Eric Cumberbatch and his like. It is this being outside the fortress of opinion that allows him and his likes to see, and to show me, what the others of our race don't and can't see.

Papa, your favourite writer Mr Rudyard Kipling seemed to understand something whereof I speak. I think he kept himself away from the poisonous attitudes of his fellow Anglo-Indians and was familiar with Indian settings, people, doings and religions. He also championed the common soldier, and I am sure approved of men who drove the trains or even stoked the engines.

Once one emerges from the confines of prejudice and the terrible snobbery that Anglo-Indians bring with them from our class-riddled, or ridden, society, one may open one's eyes to India. Remember the book by Mr Forster that Aunt Vicky forbade me to read? It is a very precious book and seems to me to address what I am here preoccupied with.

Mr Forster leaves a mystery at the heart of the novel as a young woman, Adela Quested, is conducted by an Indian doctor round an ancient cave in a hillside. She emerges with some vague accusation against the Indian doctor, and I am told that critics have puzzled over what Mr Forster meant by leaving an unexplained event in the middle of his story.

To me—and, Papa, you should read this book and confirm my opinion—it is plain that the young woman loves the Indian doctor and wants him to, yes, make love to her in the confines of the cave where the darkness can hide what she would consider sinful outside its confines. The doctor doesn't accede to her devout wish, and it leaves her desires confused. It's what India does to those who don't understand or can't fathom their own emotions.

Aunt Vicky's remarks to me and to you have been most cruel. I am in no sense ungrateful for their hospitality and their endeavour on my behalf—it was doomed from the first and had I not found this happiness of which I can now boast and content myself with, I would have felt that my life had reached its lowest point.

I beg you both to believe that I did not "elope" as she alleges or "sneak out of their house and shelter". Uncle Eb had booked my passage to England and was to accompany me on the train to the coast. He was, though they have not told you this, delayed in Poona by an important case that came up in court and couldn't accompany me. Aunt Vicky was too cross and even ill to countenance the journey, and so I was seen off at Poona station by them both and caught the Deccan Queen to Bombay.

It was, as you must have surmised, at the reversing on the ghauts that Mr Cumberbatch confronted me. I told him the whole sorry tale and he was very kind and sympathetic.

We were sitting on a promontory overlooking the valleys and talking and the mule train left before I could return. It was remiss of me and perhaps of him not to put me on that train, but there I was stranded in the country without my luggage, which had been transferred to the coaches and down to the second half of the train, which must have taken it to Victoria Terminus in Bombay. The luggage was clearly marked with the Bombay address of the Carruthers and may even now be languishing there.

He suggested that we walk along the hill road into the quaint little town of Condalla, and that was what we did. Panic had gripped me by then, and when Mr Cumberbatch suggested that we return to Poona and that I be a guest at his house for a day or two while I contemplated my future, I accepted.

He is a perfect gentleman and behaved in the most upright fashion.

Nevertheless we must have been spotted at the railway station that night when I alighted from the DQ and journeyed with him to his apartments because Uncle Eb was fairly soon informed of my return to the town and of my not having reached Bombay or taken the boat back to Blighty–Southampton.

With the help of Mr Foggerty he traced my whereabouts to Mr Eric Cumberbatch's quarters here, and a very unpleasant scene ensued. Mr Foggerty is no gentleman, and he abused my virtue and reputation in language I have never heard before, so much so that Uncle Eb threatened to horsewhip him and was compelled to drag him away, whereupon he turned on Uncle Eb and uttered the most foul accusations against him and Aunt Vicky. His demeanour became quite frightening. Was I not spared by Providence any attachment to this ghastly person?

I shall only say in conclusion that I am engaged to Eric and we shall be married as soon as I receive your blessing, or at the earliest that my disappointment will allow if I don't.

I wish I could say that he is the Director General of Indian Railways but I can't. He is one of the engine drivers of the West Coast and Southern Maratha Railways and shall be for the foreseeable future. I am content.

Your loving daughter,
Corinthia

*

The Poona Daily Gazette

17 October

The Bombay Customs and Excise Department have reported the mysterious discovery of the headless corpse of a European female among the corpses, all of them of unidentified natives which were being shipped to Rotterdam for medical dissection purposes. The macabre discovery of the corpse was made during a random check of the shipment by the Eastern Tobacco Company, which has registered this unusual cargo on several voyages since 1921.

In a further mutilation of the headless corpse, the Bombay Harbour Branch Police claim, the hands of the corpse are missing. No identification has as yet been made, and the police investigation has not turned up any lines of enquiry.

Indeed the police surgeon who was summoned to the scene claims that identification of the corpse, which has been embalmed in preservative fluid, will be very difficult and only circumstantial clues of missing European females will lead to ascertaining the identity.

⋆

The Poona Daily Gazette

28 October

The body of Mr T. Foggerty of Poona Cantt. was discovered by villagers who reported their find to the police chowkee at Lonavala. The body, the police said, had apparently been partly devoured possibly by hyenas or other scavenging animals of the Western Ghats. Mr Foggerty was an employee of the Eastern Tobacco Company engaged in their export trade.

Assistant Commander Willis of Poona Cantt. told reporters that Mr Foggerty had been murdered by three bullet wounds to the head and that his body had been dumped next to the Bombay-Poona railway tracks by the murderer or murderers. The murder weapon has not been recovered.

Mr Foggerty's funeral will take place at 10 a.m. on the 18th inst. at St. Mary's Church, Race Course Road, Poona Cantt.

⋆

(*A correspondence added to the First Edition. – fd*)

From: gbmdeshmukh@gmail.com
To: prisonerofpoonaFdhondy@gmail.com

Dear Mr Dhondy,

I have obtained your e-mail from your publishers and want to ask you one question about your one episode in your novel *Deccan Queen*. It is a very engaging book, sir, and I don't mean to distract from its excellence or cast any shadows on your brilliant and fluid command of English. In fact we are very proud in Pune that a boy born and educated in our town, in our famous schools and colleges is now a published author of books and other things.

However, I would beg to ask you where you obtained the ideas or evidence for the episode which you have labelled in the book "Indian Passages". I am somewhat intrigued on particular accounts by the events thereof. Please cast some enlightenment on your sources.

Your reader, fan and critic,
Prof. Gangadhar B.M. Deshmukh
Pune University

*

To: gbmdeshmukh@gmail.com

Dear Prof. Deshmukh,

Thank you for your e-mail and your kind remarks.

In answer to your question about the particular section of *Deccan Queen*, I stumbled quite by chance on the diaries of the young lady whom I have called Corinthia Greenford. It's a much more romantic name than she actually had and I have based the episode on the characters I encountered there. The diaries are in the possession of a personal friend of the family to which the young lady belonged.

Hope that answers your query.

Best wishes,
Farrukh Dhondy

*

To: prisonerofpoona@gamil.com

I am grateful for your e-mail reply, but I wish to point out some things to you which contradict the fact that you extracted this story from the memoirs of a real person existing and travelling in 1931 recorded in the diary of the same year.

I am, as my hobby and partly professional interest, somewhat familiar with the history of Indian railways. I am sorry to say there is plenty of erroneous material in the episode as you have depicted it.

I am delineating the mistakes, sir:

First of all, the Deccan Queen never was running with a steam engine. By the time the Deccan Queen was on tracks, the railway between Mumbai and Pune had introduced electrical modern engines. On occasion these were supplemented to carry the excess load by diesel-fuelled engines.

The other very puzzling fact is the talk of the Reversing and the mule trains that came down the non-rail conveyance passages of the Western Ghats. Sir, the Indian railways and the tracks that they engineered have been going since 1840 and by the time the Deccan Queen came into service 90 years later, the rail track between Kalyan and Khandala traversing the entire mountain range of the Western Ghats had been constructed.

By the year 1931, the "Reversing" as you call it in your book was known to us locals as "the old reversing" as no trains reversed there anymore but carried on down the Ghats and perhaps paused at a station we call Monkey Hill to test the brakes!

There could have been no mule conveyance for your Miss Corinthia and there could have been no romantic encounters at the changeover in Khandala because the journey of the Deccan Queen was unimpeded and continuous up and down the mountain.

I feel it necessary to bring these matters to your attention and do not doubt that you have based the episode on some lady's memory as presented in diaries, but beg to differ on above-mentioned facts.

Why don't you eliminate the name Deccan Queen from this episode and change all the dates to around 1919.

Your supporter, though critic,
Prof. G. Deshmukh

*

To: gbmdeshnukh@gmail.com

Dear Prof. Deshmukh,

My book is a work of fiction and doesn't have to stick very strictly to the history of the railways in India. Perhaps I invented the steam engine, and the mule rides were certainly there down the mountains. Your suggestion of 1919 will not work for readers of literature though it works for railway historians, because I mention Forster's *A Passage to India* and it wasn't published then.

So I thank you for your attention and can we say the matter is closed? Fiction—not claiming to transgress or deny your mastery of the facts or rail history?

Ever,
fd

*

To: prisonerofpoona@gamil.com

Mr Dhondy,

I very much doubt if you are in possession of any diaries from that era at all. You are claiming in your so-called story that some dead bodies from Indian streets are being sold abroad for experimentation by medical institutions. This is disgracing the Indian nation by saying we are selling our human flesh as if our glorious country has nothing else to trade.

This is a shameful claim and not worthy of someone who calls himself an Indian. I enclose for your attention an article I have written about your so-called book to the *Pune Pioneer* outlining this very point. I am sure you must have missed it by living abroad so I am enclosing for your attention.

With best wishes,
Prof. G.B.M. Deshmukh

⋆

To
The Editor,
Pune Pioneer

Sir,

Professor Deshmukh's ill-tempered attack on Farrukh Dhondy's *Deccan Queen* is wide of the mark. What Mr Dhondy is saying doesn't bring shame on India but on the British administration of the time which presided over the poverty and degrading conditions which allowed dead bodies to be picked up by profiteers of the colonial companies. At least one of the bodies, if you read carefully Professorji, is not an Indian but a white person.

The blame is clearly on the villain of his piece, one Mr Foggerty who by his name and profession has to be English. The company for which he works carries on this trade and it is their shame and disgrace and not the person's who has pointed this out.

I remain, etc.
K.J. Ramamurthi
Atomic Research Commission
Pune

*

From The Editor,
Rumor Books

Farrukh,
Why don't you correct the dates of this story as suggested by the good Prof. who took the trouble to write to you? I understand your reply and the fictionalisation entailing Forster's *Passage* which was published in 1924, so you can easily date the events of the episode in that year. And of course the train need not be the Deccan Queen but some predecessor. Do tell me what you decide ASAP because we've already announced the second edition in our catalogue.

Best,
Miriam

*

To
The Editor
Pune Pioneer

Sir,

Professor Deshmukh may be in complete command of the facts and history of railway lines and perhaps timetables but it doesn't qualify him to venture into literary territory.

His remarks about Dhondy's text, *Deccan Queen*, are misconceived and demonstrate an unfamiliarity with the interpretation of modern literature. To put it as politely as I can, he has handled Dhondy's supreme text as a monkey would a computer. He doesn't know what it's for or what to do with it.

The text under discussion is a supreme example of the subaltern acquisition of postmodern discourse. The hybridisation of the faux-naif detective genre with the Lacanian dislocation of time and idiom is, I would submit, unique. The particular sequential exposition to which Professor Deshmukh objects has a Borgesian quality in that it leaves a disappearance and a murder unsolved and yet convincingly solved.

The dislocated date and technology to which Deshmukh points are deliberate narrative strategies to generate the uncertainties of the conclusion. Deshmukh's objections amount to saying that Picasso is "mistaken" in having painted a woman with two noses.

I remain respectfully,
K.K. Barua
Professor of Literature
Ahmednagar University

*

Miriam,

Have enclosed a letter from the *Pune Pioneer* which replies decisively to Professor Deshmukh's objections which you seem to be bothered by.

Farrukh

*

Farrukh,

The letter is a load of nonsense and you know it is. You're just being stubborn and lazy and refuse to change the dates or the name of the train. Did you write that silly letter yourself? I have checked and there is no such Professor at Ahmednagar University. In fact there's no such university!

Best wishes and some annoyance,
Miriam

A Trapdoor

In 1962 there was a flood in Poona. The dam across a lake in Khadakvasla held the water supply of the city and in heavy rain, when the sluices of this dam had rusted and couldn't be opened to let the pressure of the water into the river, the dam burst. The river flowed over its banks through the city and swept away everything for hundreds of yards on either side of its bank. Houses, huts, slums, bridges, cattle sheds and the riverside granaries that stored the city's grain.

The dead cattle and the rotting grain on the banks as the flood receded gave off a smell that permeated the city. It was the smell of death, and it was everywhere and all-pervasive.

Leaving Poona two years after the flood, when the debris that it had caused had been cleared up and the smell was gone, it returned to my nostrils as a memory. Was I escaping from the—yes—terror of that stink that had drowned the city? Was I, leaving for Bombay now and for the unknown adventure of England, escaping the enclosing smallness of the town I grew up in?

Though I wanted to leave, there was inevitably a feeling of dread. Of venturing into the unknown.

Should I be nostalgic for the town that brought me up? Did I feel that nostalgia already as the train pulled away from the platform with a whistle?

In crowded, thronging, bustling Bombay one expected to look into that abyss. On its streets I looked into the sockets of hollow eyes and thought I saw the grey, breathing, fungus-covered membrane of the brain. I saw faces falling off their skulls, dogs literally foraging in the entrails of dogs and looking up with guilty, protective eyes, blood round their jaws like the painted mouths of clowns in the tattered circus rigged on the maidans…

We denizens of Poona, we came and went on the Deccan Queen. Went this time! Forever? On the Deccan Queen.

*

(*Added to this chapter of the First Edition. – fd*)

From my iPhone

Mr Dhondy, you are a bastard and fool living in UK and writing dirty things about glorious cities like Pune and Mumbai. Why don't you say something filthy about your own dirty cities like Karachi and Lahore where pavements are running with blood?

LION OF BHARAT

From my iPhone

Dear Lion of Bharat-ji. I assume you conclude from my first name that I am a Pakistani Muslim. It's an idiotic conclusion. I was born a Parsi Zoroastrian and am very much an Indian. My patriotism, unlike yours, is international—*phir bhi dil hein Hindustani*, Lion sahib! Now fuck off!

fd

Yes Yes Yes!

And for our next question, ladies and gentlemen, what is the Deccan Queen?

Is it:

a) a multi-layered Indian fast-food sandwich

b) an ancient Amazon of Southern India, revered today for her miraculous power of granting any wish of escape?

c) a gay person with Decca's syndrome?

d) a character from some Kiplingesque, Lewis Carroll fantasy called Alisha in Wonderland?

But haven't I already told you what it is?

Timetabled to go from Poona early each morning and return from Bombay at night, in time for a meal and bed. Past Lonavala, past Khandala, the last post on the cliffs, chugging through tunnels of highland, down from the plateau, the mud-brown train, to the scattered palms and brackish waters with clumps of residual swamp on the coastal strip and the first scattered concrete buildings and then the relentless suburbs, oblivious of this daily rite of passage in their backyard, to the blackened and ancient embankments of the ever-crumbling heart of the city.

All too real city, India's great metaphor of indifference. For me a city of farewells. With always the promise to return, but in another incarnation, when life and fortune have changed you, changed this habitation to another city, its map and people different, its familiar landmarks only part of its mockery of your return.

The Deccan Queen was the connection between two worlds. The simplest pairing was that of the quiet plateau town of Poona and the busy coastal city of Bombay. The deeper but still simple connection would be the peace of one and the threatened nightmare of the other. Innocence and experience. Determined paths and imagined opportunities. The link to the world as it had become with all its wonders. The vehicle of damnation. The real frontier. Bombay was, prosaically, where the airport was, where the trains to Delhi or Calcutta went from.

The Deccan Queen was to a boy in Poona a "Get out of jail free" card. No, not free! There was always the price.

To the colonials of the Raj it was the swift connection between two worlds. Here was the continent of Circe with great promises of spices, trade, fortunes, the sweltering, damp, never-relenting heat of the coastal city and the cool of the plateau of Poona. The sahibs and memsahibs lived in the two worlds of India—the administrative hubs of Delhi and Calcutta and the summer capital of Simla in the lower Himalayas. And here the men who work them and some idiots who spot them fall in love with trains.

*

(Miriam, nothing to add to this chapter for the Second Edition as no one responded or reacted. – fd)

Puk Puk Puk Puk Pukkaaka Puk

From the age of six or so till I was twenty and left for England, I lived with my mother's family—her two unmarried sisters, my grandfather and for several years my grandmother's older sister, my grandaunt, who was crippled with arthritis and had been brought from Bombay to live with us in the half of the city bungalow that the family occupied.

The ceilings of this tiled sloping-roofed, shabby dwelling were high, and at the top of the outer wall of each room was a ventilator window, which could be manoeuvred open by a rope that hung from a primitive pulley system. This kept the air in and the sparrows out or let the risen warm air out and the sparrows in to nest in the corners of the wooden slatted ceiling.

The rooms followed from a front veranda one after the other. The veranda led into a sitting room with sofas and a proud, wooden-cased radiogram and the portraits of ancestors on the walls. There was a bookcase with the works of Gandhi, Kahlil Gibran and the *Oxford Book of Modern Verse* along with the works of Erle Stanley Gardner from a comprehensive reading of which I learned to repeat "incompetent, irrelevant and immaterial" to annoy opponents in argument.

The first room led to three successive bedrooms, the first with three beds for my aunts and grandaunt, then my grandfather's room and then the wardrobes and two beds of the room I shared with my sister, which opened out on to a side veranda that contained my study table, chair, lamp and small cupboard to partition off the area and store my work files and texts.

Our trusty old maid, Chandri, who had looked after my aunts when they were young and was now part of the family and household, used the side veranda as her bedroom, and beyond where she slept was an old leather suitcase full of musty-smelling discarded clothes, which we as children would pull out and wear as costume.

The furthermost room at the back of the house was the dining room with its table, fridge and meat-safe, a little closet with metal grille doors, and the red terracotta urn on its metal tripod from which the family drank the cooled, muslin-strained water that the cook poured into it each morning.

From the dining room, steps led to the small back veranda with a basin over which was a mirror that was embossed in large print with the words "STOLEN FROM WESTERN RAILWAYS". My uncle, who lived in Bombay, insisted he bought it from a second-hand furniture shop, either as a piece of mischief or at a discount he couldn't resist. The back veranda opened into a small yard with a little brick kitchen hut on the side and a small dark-tiled hut against the back wall in which we kept the stock of wood that was burnt each morning in a large speckled metal boiler to make hot water for our bucket baths.

The entire house, the yard, the verandas and the sloping roof was half of the bungalow, which was divided down its spine, with a mirror-image dwelling running parallel from the street entrance and front veranda to the wood-stocking "godown" as we called it. Only the family that occupied the Siamese-twinned house didn't use the godown as a wood storage space but as an outhouse servants' quarters.

The two small backyards were divided by a wall on either side of which grew a mango tree. Our mango tree, though distinctly of the same breed, was sterile and bore no fruit, but the neighbour's tree gave forth each year and when the mangoes were green and small, served me and my friends for target practice with our .177 DIANA air rifles. It was a thoughtless pastime as the lead pellets of the mangoes we hit stayed embedded and ruined the mangoes as they ripened. When they were harvested and Mr Minocher Toot, the patriarch of the neighbouring family, supervised the plucking of the fruit, he would find his precious stock damaged and a portion of it ruined.

The complaints would be issued to the families of all the boys in the neighbourhood who hung around our backyard, and the colourful abuse would pour over the back wall. Not in mine, but in several families whose fathers were friends of Mr Toot, a flogging might follow the complaints. My grandfather would confiscate the airgun and lock it away in his steel cupboard for several months till compassion overtook him. By the time the next crop of mangoes were budding, he would have forgotten.

One of the games of skill we played was to try and hit the stems of the damaged mangoes with pellets and drop them before the damage was detected on harvest day.

The mangoes were plucked by a little monkey of a lad, the servant of Mr Minocher Toot, who would in his khaki shorts clamber up to the outlying branches, which mostly hung over and sheltered our yard. He was called Yeshwant. He would sit on the highest branch that would hold his weight, pluck the mangoes and throw them into the next yard where Minocher Toot and one of his sons or his maid, one Saibai, would hold up a bedsheet into which the fruit would be projected to cushion its fall.

We made it a practice to pay off Yeshwant before harvest day to examine the mangoes damaged by lead pellets and let them drop into our part of the yard "by mistake". He was paid in sweets, marbles and money and was always willing to take what he could, driving a hard bargain on occasion and, we suspected, letting a few damaged mangoes through to the bedsheet to where old Toot could find them just to maintain the equity of crime and punishment in our world.

Yeshwant was not a happy boy. He slept on the back veranda of Toot's half of the house and was regularly beaten by the master with a thick wooden rod encased in leather, a sort of military swagger-stick. He would be beaten for work not done, for loitering at the corner of the street when he was sent out for bottles of soda, for puncturing the tyres of the bicycle and once even for falling from the mango tree on harvest day. But looking at him you wouldn't know that he was unhappy, because apart from shouting and weeping through the beatings and for a few minutes after, he was always grinning from ear to ear and singing little Marathi ditties as he scrubbed the cooking vessels under the yard tap.

He had been in the service of that family for years. He came from a village outside Poona, somewhere between our town and Bombay, and had been delivered by an uncle to work in that household. The neighbour's boys said that Yeshwant was a thief and not to be trusted and had been disowned by his family because he was caught stealing in the village and had escaped the wrath of the villagers by being smuggled out by the uncle who brought him to their household.

He was a few years younger than myself, and we occasionally talked across the yard wall when he would utter a lot of gibberish, making fun of our ability to speak in English. He would parody the lilt quite accurately without the vocabulary to make it satirical.

"See bot krish may collpish golasten, fish fosh?" he would say as though asking a question, a grin all over his face.

I would on occasion reply in Marathi and tell him that if he didn't make their saucepans shine he would get a beating, and I would take sadistic pleasure in listening to his howls.

"Looky chweet zanterkofield, sublaysam, fish fosh!" he would say.

His English sentences always ended in "fish fosh".

If we met in the street outside our house he would talk sensibly. He would ask how I was and how much the new bicycle he observed my sister riding cost and whether Indian bicycles, though they were heavier, were actually sturdier than foreign ones. He might ask if I could give him empty lemonade bottles to sell to the "dabba-batliwallis", our local recycling operatives, women who walked down the street with baskets on their heads and bought old newspapers by the weight and old bottles by the number. If I said we had a few old soda bottles or whatever, he would ask me to slip them to him when Saibai, the maid of their household, was not around lest she demand her percentage.

Not that Saibai had any need for the small sums the sale of waste would bring. She had a good thing going. She was hired as a cook and domestic servant by Mrs Toot, a Parsi lady in her fifties who had grown prematurely white and spent most of the day in the house in her flowered cotton nightgowns supervising the coming and going of the dhobi, the egg-woman, the milkman with his buffaloes, the man who refluffed the cotton wool in mattresses and pillows with a cat-gut and wood bow before stitching the mattress up again, the rat-catchers and assorted tradesmen whose services were essential to a household's life.

Saibai had been assigned the detached room at the end of their yard and sat on its step a few times a week oiling and combing her long black hair. She was, for a Maratha woman, fairish-skinned, and she had wide, thin lips and very snaky eyes. As the months passed her domestic duties fell away and she would enter the house less and less, sticking to the kitchen where she prepared food, to the yard where she preened herself and to her room where she would, when they thought no one had noticed, receive hour-long or half-hour-long visits from Mr Minocher Toot.

Their privacy was a vain conceit. Yeshwant was aware of everything that went on in the household. The children of the house were either at college or out at work in the daytime, and if Mrs Toot went out visiting and the house was left to Mr Toot, who had a sort of workshop and called himself an "inventor", and to Saibai, Mr Toot would seize the hour and the two of them would seclude themselves in her little dark room.

Yeshwant at first kept his counsel, kept their secret. He must have been threatened by Toot and would have taken heed. Until the day when Mrs Toot returned unexpectedly from visiting a very sick friend, who had been discharged from the hospital and taken to Bombay, and found the house open and Mr Toot not at his inventions. She was no fool. She went to the backyard and finding no Saibai in the kitchen and the crooked but thick wooden door to the servant's room shut, she went and rattled the five-linked chain that hung from the lintel to lock the door from the outside and shouted for Saibai.

There was, unsurprisingly, no answer.

"Saibai, I know you are in there. You left the daal next to the stove and it's still hot. Come out. Come out now."

She turned round. My grandaunt, hearing the commotion and knowing exactly what was going on, left her lunch on the dining table and shuffled to the doorway at the top of the back veranda steps from where she could see Mrs Toot desperately rattling the chain and calling out.

I was at my books, it being examination week in school, and hearing the commotion went round the back to the yard.

My grandaunt dodged back into the dining room. She didn't want to embarrass Mrs Toot further. And poor Mrs Toot turned and saw Yeshwant standing behind her at a distance with an insolent grin.

"Where is the master?" Mrs Toot demanded.

Yeshwant made no answer, but his grin was enough. Now the woman was distraught.

"Minocher, Minocher," she shouted.

She pronounced the name with a stylish flourish even in her distress. Most couples would have abbreviated the classical Persian name to the mundane "Meenu" but not Mrs Toot, who maintained the idea that she was of a certain class.

"Why are you doing this to me, Minocher?" she screamed.

Answer came there none.

Now our cook, one Hukam Ali, and our maid had been alerted to the commotion, and we stood in embarrassed, silent, attentive stances, till my grandfather, appearing at the back door, careless of whether Mrs Toot could hear him, shouted at us to get back to our work and to mind our various businesses.

"Minocher, I will sit here till you come out with your bitch. I swear I will not move, even if I starve to death here and you starve to death inside with your whore," she said.

I waited till my grandfather had retreated and then returned to peer at this unexpected drama. I was twelve years old.

Mrs Toot hung on to the iron chain and rattled it now and again at the silence within.

Were they pretending they weren't there and hoping she would go away? She repeated his name over and over again, and she began to cry. Then, unaware that I could see her and careless of the silent Yeshwant who stood in the yard still grinning, she lifted the hem of the nightdress into which she must have changed to preserve her hospital-visiting sari and dried her eyes. I could see her knickers and her hairy legs, and I stared at them and felt guilty for not turning away.

She was true to her word. She sat there for five hours and then rattling the chain reminded Minocher that their sons would be back soon and they would break down the door, which she had vainly and feebly shouldered.

"Minocher, come out with your whore. The boys will be back any minute, and if you come out now I won't say anything to them. If you stay inside they will know, and when they come I will scream like a woman whose children have all died."

She continued to sob and to dry her tears and bare her hairy legs and crotch.

It was the first time I had heard or seen anyone offer this sort of gambit—her silence for an admission and for the emergence of the adulterer and adulteress.

It worked. Saibai emerged combing her long tresses, with a sly smile as though she were preening herself after a long encounter. There was no touch of shame but only provocation in the way she looked at the tear-stained and haggard Mrs Toot. Mr Toot opened the wooden door, stepped out, frowning as though he was the aggrieved party and without a word to his wife went into their house.

"And I want her dismissed, now, or I'll tell them," she shouted after him.

It was an empty threat, and he didn't respond. She followed him into the house. Saibai grinned and showed her one gold tooth.

That's when Yeshwant started his singing. He went to the tap in the yard and turning it on, put his hand under the faucet and forced the vertical stream of water into a horizontal fanning spray, which went all over the yard to wet the ground and cool it. And he began to sing:

"Puk puk puk puk pukaaka puk
Jhalee maajee kamchi rakh!"

The first line was rendered in imitation of a clucking chicken and the second, which is Marathi for "my work is ruined, fucked, screwed", almost joyfully.

The sons of the house returned from their study and their jobs, chained their bicycles to the wrought-iron banisters of the veranda, took off the bicycle clips they wore on the hems of their trousers to prevent them getting caught in the chain and shouted to Saibai, the cook, to get them their tea. But Saibai, sitting on the step of her servant's room, making herself a paan from a little brass chest full of red and white pastes and crushed betel nut, paid no heed. Instead she turned her head and spat the residue of betel-leaf from her mouth.

Her position in the household had changed. She may have been the mistress of the Master for a long time before, but being discovered was in a sense being acknowledged. Her concubinage had been exposed, and she was no longer the skivvy making tea.

Mrs Toot realized this at the same moment and went into the kitchen to put the kettle on their coal stove to make her sons the tea they had called for. She didn't look at Saibai, who watched her, going into the kitchen and emerging with the teapot, as the Cheshire cat might have watched a bird she couldn't be bothered to pounce on.

Yeshwant sang his *puk puk puk puk pukaaka puk* song, and for him it marked not the ruin of his work, but a retirement from it. His relationship with the Master was forever altered. He still climbed the mango tree each season, and he watered the plants, hosed the yard and ran errands, but Mr Toot didn't dare beat him anymore and even bought him a second-hand bicycle of which Yeshwant was very proud.

When the sons of the family were out, there were terrible fights between Mr and Mrs Toot as he was now expelled from the marital bed and asserted his mastery of the house by slipping into Saibai's shabby boudoir with sulky impunity whenever he chose. She would be waiting for him inside, appearing in the doorway in her choli and the long limp skirt-like sari petticoat she had recently taken to wearing. It was one more touch of her elevation to memsahib status as Maratha women of her caste and class wore their saris without petticoats into which to tuck them. She now dressed as rich Parsi or other middle-class women would.

Mrs Toot would avoid the yard but cry in the doorway. She retained her gentility in the face of this brutality. My grandfather never spoke of what was going on, but he would shut the big double doors of the dining room to preserve our household from the shameful sights and sounds from the neighbouring yard.

Yeshwant would carry on as though nothing was happening, and the repeated sound of *puk puk puk puk pukaaka puk* would tell us that it was.

Then Mrs Toot fell ill, and she must have told the sons of the household what had been troubling her and how her heart had been broken, and Saibai was dismissed and disappeared. Mr Toot sulked like a big smelly bear, and neither his wife nor his sons talked to him except to tell him to have a bath. He took to wearing absurd plastic dark glasses, which he had "invented", whilst taking an evening stroll with his walking stick. In the neighbourhood the story went that he had installed Saibai in a room somewhere in the City and that was the reason he insisted on taking solitary walks through crowded streets where no one taking a constitutional evening stroll would venture.

Yeshwant's grinning blackmail must also have come to the attention of the sons of the household because he too disappeared. A deal must have been struck because he took the second-hand bicycle with him.

Let thirty years pass. Let me forget about Yeshwant, Saibai and the enterprising Mr Toot and his tragic wife as I move away from Poona, from India and through foreign universities and jobs and with some difficulty make a career in writing and in film and television. I work for a UK television channel, commission a parcel of Indian documentaries for it and land up in Bombay to supervise, assist with and interfere in their making.

One of the documentaries is about the political and social change that has swept Bombay in the previous thirty years, since I used to travel from Poona on the Deccan Queen to the City of Lure.

Ever on the lookout for the dramatic story, however hurtful and negative, the director who is working for me alights on the fact that the Marathi-chauvinist, provincially minded political party, the Shiv Brigade, have attacked, wounded and reputedly killed taxi drivers and other workers who come from the northern Indian states. The story of the victims of this pogrom has been told in all the news items, and my TV team resolves to delve into the story from the other side. Without any inclination to sympathize with murdering marauders, they want to understand how they arrived at a position that should be anathema to citizens in a proud, young but prosperous democracy.

The crew is to film a Shiv Brigade rally whose speakers will undoubtedly attempt to justify their stance of physically attacking humble and defenceless workers who are Indian citizens working perfectly legally in an Indian city.

I go along. For an hour before we get to the maidan where the rally is being held, the throngs of the Sena, the audience the rally has attracted or commanded, clog the streets and pass along the pavements, some in organized groups chanting slogans as they move. Through "contacts", as is the rule in India, our crew has secured rights to shoot the speakers from close-up and the rally from a vantage point.

We are brought chairs and shown the utmost courtesy. The rally is ready to applaud each demagogue, each Robespierre who mounts the platform. And yes, it's him. There is no mistaking, after thirty years, the widow's peak of the hairline and the thick lips that break into the same grin when a joke of his, a piece of sarcasm against the prime minister, is applauded for a full thirty seconds.

After the speeches we are to interview a spokesman for the Sena at a five-star hotel. I go along. It is him. He is sitting in an air-conditioned lounge reserved for the purpose with four or five attendants who tell us, even as he listens and frowns, that their district chief, or whatever title they give him, is tired after the rally, and we shall have to be very brief. He sits in a fresh white kurta into which he has now changed and wears dark glasses. He is clutching a handkerchief in his right hand, for the effect he can create when he gestures with it.

I am introduced, and he knits his brow when he hears my name. He wrenches his dark glasses off. He is handsome. He breaks into a grin. He speaks in English with a clear accent. He has acquired the language and suave manner on the way.

"I can't believe it," he says. "Is it really?"

"I'm afraid so," I say.

"No," he says. "Same name maybe?"

It's a game.

"Same person. I suppose I have to prove it," I say.

He grins.

"*Puk puk puk puk pukaaka puk*," I say.

He knew that was coming.

"So you've come with your foreign TV crew to call us murderers and fascists and to fuck our work, have you?"

"Yes," I say.

He clicks his fingers to the rhythm he invented so many years ago.

"*Jhalee majee kamchi rakh!*"

He corrects my Marathi. "*Jhali mahjye kamachi rakh*," he responds and grins.

*

(*Response added to the Second Edition. – fd*)

The Times of India

Mumbai, 30 June: *The office of Shiv Brigade Leader Yeshwantrao Marathwada claims that the author of a recently published novel titled* Deccan Queen *has featured him in it and seriously libelled him. The press release threatens to sue Mr F. Dhondy, the author, and his publisher and editors for libel. Mr Marathwada has already issued a notice alleging slander to the TV News Channel KHABAR for the interview they did with the author and publishers in which a passage from the book was read out alleging that Mr Marathwada began life as a humble servant boy and used his knowledge of scandals in the household to resort to blackmail.*

The allegations in the story which was read and discussed on the TV channel gave rise to several taunting questions from Mr Marathwada's rivals within the Shiv Brigade organisation and there were calls for his resignation from the secretariat of the party and from the Police Scrutiny Commission recently set up by the party leadership.

Mr Devrao Patil, who stood in the secretarial elections of the party against Mr Marathwada, told this newspaper that "we can't have a person who has allegedly been involved in thieving and blackmailing activities involved in our investigation of the corruption of the police. We are the party of clean hands and of national pride in our identity and heritage and this sort of allegation rolling out of a prominent member's past has to be cleared up before he can be embraced into the spheres of responsibility. I am sure that the allegations made by these freelance writers are totally without basis, but that must be now put to the test, otherwise or by strenuous investigations and a clearing of the faulty and no-doubt erroneous charge-sheet by Mr Marathwada himself."

*

From: AnilDDDD@gmail.com
To: fdhondy@lucidwriting.co.uk

Farrukh Sahib,

Meri jaan, what the fuck have you gone and done now? Your book may not be *Anna Karenina* but is selling like chewing gum here in NY. But get down to business: A millionaire of my acquaintance, a Maharashtrian who lives in NY part of the time and is a strong supporter and financier of the Shiv Brigade, wants a favour. He knows I know you and says he is very upset at what you have written about Yeshwant Marathwada who is heading for great things in Indian politics. He can't tolerate the sort of glitch you have introduced though I am sure when you are sued you will provide evidence in court and prove that you are right about poor sneaky Yeshwant.

Nevertheless, my man here is willing to get Yeshu (who is dependent on him for cash) to withdraw all charges of libel against you if you will recant! All you need to do is to write in the Indian newspapers or give an interview saying that the story is completely fictional and that you will change the ending in a future edition and something to the effect that the Yeshwant in your story is NOT Mr Marathwada whom you don't know from Adam. My man is willing to pay you $10,000 to do this little thing.

Now don't be stubborn. Remember Galileo?

Xox
Anil

*

From: fdhondy@lucidwriting.co.uk
To: AnilDDDD@gmail.com

Anil jaan,

What the fuck! You too, Brute! 30 pieces? Mess of pottage? I can't believe your e-mail. You want me to write a column in the Indian national papers denouncing myself for something I wrote? I told it like it was!

Please old man—how much did your anonymous "Man" pay you to put this outrageous proposal to me? You can't have joined the fascist party or be working for them. Remember marching through the streets of Poona shouting, "Hamara naam, thoomara naam, Vietnam, Vietnam!"—how can soup turn to slurry? It was a joke, yeah?

X
f

*

From: AnilDDDD@gmail.com
To: fdhondy@lucidwriting.co.uk

Arsehole,

It's not a joke! And I haven't turned fascist. I am in New York, duh, and am revaluing the equation between literary conceits and hard cash! I live in the Great Satan, remember? I was passing on a proposal from the Man who is willing to raise the stakes to $14000 maybe (and I, being an impoverished hack myself, get a cut, right?).

Dude, it's a simple fucking thing to do. What do your publishers pay you? Crap? Fish and chips for a week in London or battered deep-fried Mars bars in Scotland? I know that writers think the truth is precious. It's not—truth is cash because it pays the rent. And I bet you made half of that shit up anyway. (Hey, I loved the book, eh, and thanks for putting me in it. Show it to my grandchildren. Or maybe you'll cut me out in the next edition!)

You don't mention the deal—like Mother Teresa you are only ranting on about my soul. Come down from there, baby.

OK, don't write a column, give an interview to a big paper or to my paper and say the same thing. Collect $10 big ones as you pass GO and do not go to jail for criminal libel. They'll put you away, baby, they have the courts eating out of their hands.

X
aDDDD

*

The Times of India

Mumbai, 5 July: *The internecine wars in the Shiv Brigade came to a head and to blows at the Central Committee meeting at Shiv Bhavan Lower Parel today when Mr Yeshawant Marathwada was replaced by Mr Devrao Patil as General Secretary of the party after a vote of no confidence was passed and a fresh election ordered by the Chairperson Mrs Suhashini Kamble. One committee member, Mr Wadidar Hemlikar, challenged Mrs Kamble's right to call an election. The chair ignored his challenge and proceeded with the vote amid cries from the meeting of corruption and purchased votes. It was alleged that Mr Patil's faction had bribed seventeen committee members with houses in the areas they controlled in Mumbai and other districts.*

Fisticuffs were thrown as the vote was taken and in the general melee the police were summoned. Seven arrests were made, and after, the floor was cleared and the meeting adjourned.

It is expected that Mr Marathwada and his faction will resign from the SB and form a new party which may carry the majority of voters with it particularly after the allegation three years ago of Mr Patil's implication in the murder of his brother and his marriage to his brother's widow though no allegation of wrongdoing has ever been proved against Mr Patil.

Nevertheless, according to the opinion polls of this newspaper at the time and in the latest poll, Mr Patil's popularity has suffered as a result of the scandal that followed his brother's alleged suicide and it is rock bottom with women members who constitute thirty-three per cent of all membership. The female membership was the result of a drive by Mr Marathwada's faction in 2010 and Mr Marathwada has always boasted that the percentage of female members of his party is greater than that of any other popular and general political party in the country.

⋆

Extract from *The Daily Age*

IN AN EXCLUSIVE INTERVIEW WITH ANIL DHAWAN, FARRUKH DHONDY WITHDRAWS ALLEGATIONS HE MADE IN HIS NOVEL 'DECCAN

QUEEN' AGAINST SB LEADER YESHWANTRAO MARATHWADA

Anil: So the whole story you called "Puk-puk-puk-puk" in your book is a fiction and none of it is true?

Dhondy: Of course, it's a complete fiction and the nature of fiction is that it's not true.

Anil: It's a good story, but which bit of it is untrue?

Dhondy: All of it, except the description of my house. That's taken from reality, but there were no such neighbours and no such servants. Saibai is a fictional character, and the boy servant Yeshwant is made up. He never existed.

Anil: And the politician at the end of the story?

Dhondy: That is a fabrication to round off the plot.

Anil: So the name Yeshwant is a coincidence and nothing to do with Mr Marathwada of the SB?

Dhondy: Look, Anil, thousands of men are called Yeshwant. I plucked a name out of the air. Of course, it has nothing to do with Mr Marathwada whom I have never met. If my story has caused him any distress I take this opportunity to apologize.

Anil: What do you mean if it has caused him distress? Your story was used as evidence in an internal party meeting and in faction fighting to dislodge him from important positions. What do you say to that?

Dhondy: I can only repeat my apology and hope that party members will note that they were deceived into thinking that my invention had anything to do with Mr Marathwada.

Anil: Thank you, Farrukh, that's very clear.

*

From: prisonerofpoona@gamil.com
To: AnilDDDD@gmail.com

Anil, you fucking bastard! How could you do that? I suppose you knew that I wouldn't take you or your rag of a newspaper to court for fabricating an interview with me. Didn't it once cross your mercenary mind that we have known each other since we were six and that's a really filthy thing to do. What does it make me look like? I've written to your wretched editor who could have checked with me, telling him I never gave you any interview and you made it all up, but I'm sure you've stepped on him to bin the letter and not publish it. I can of course give an interview to another paper.

I suppose you think it's a laugh. I will go to the fire temple now and pray that your prick falls off and that one of the famous rats of New York makes a tiny morsel of it!

Your 'friend'
F---ing outrage'd.

*

From: AnilDDDD@gmail.com
To: fdhondy@lucidwriting.co.uk

Darling f,

Glad you took it well. Put yourself in my position! Read it over when you stop boiling and cool down—it only says you are a great fiction writer and not a mere reporter like the rest of us.

Send your bank details—your $5000 is on its way.

Xox
aDDDD

*

Miscellaneous headlines from *The Daily Age*

YM REINSTATED AS GENERAL SECRETARY OF THE SB

PATIL FACTION BREAKS WITH SB AND ANNOUNCES FORMATION OF CHHATRAPATI SENA (CS)

*

From: prisonerofpoona@gamil.com
To: AnilDDDD@gmail.com

A,

Thanks for the cash transfer even if it was only 50%. Am "rewriting" or republishing a second edition of *Deccan Queen* with additions of all the correspondence and reactions. I am sure your (our?) patron will find it interesting,

Love as always,
f

Deccan Queen Installed

Stuart McKay came to Bombay by cargo steamer in early 1929. The ship came from Liverpool, round the Bay of Biscay, past Gib, through the Med and Suez, refuelling in Aden and so to India's best harbour. The steamer was carrying the undercarriages of the "rakes", the passenger coaches destined to be the body of the fastest electric train in Imperial India, made by Metropolitan Cammell Coach and Wagon Works of Birmingham where McKay was chief fitting engineer.

He had very little to do with the construction of the undercarriages, the rolling stock of the train. That was not the engineering speciality that the firm used him for, though he was perfectly equipped, having studied at Glasgow University, to assess and design such undercarriages. No, McKay was Cammell C&W's expert in the design requirements and fitting of the car bodies and coach work that were manufactured and were to be assembled at the Matunga Carriage and Wagon Works in Bombay.

Matunga at the time was a fairly new industrial site, north of Dadar and Parel, with their older nineteenth-century dark, fairly satanic fabric mills on the Bombay island/peninsula. McKay and two other engineers had supervised the transport of the undercarriages, the main frame of a new train, which was to be the first electrified link between Calyan and Poona. Calyan, now Kalyan, is down on the coastal strip from which spring the Western Ghats.

The climb up the ghats is steep and dangerous, and the laying of a railway up these mountains, with nearly thirty tunnels cut through the black volcanic rock, requires powerful engines. Steam couldn't do it, but now that the line was electrified, the Great Indian Peninsula Railway would run its new train first from Calyan to Poona as a trial of the mountain segment and then extend it to Bombay so that the sahibs whose memsahibs lived in the cooler and less sticky climate of Poona could commute to Bombay for the working week and back to Poona for the weekends.

The new train, it was planned, would run on weekends only, going from Bombay's Victoria Terminus to Poona on a Friday evening and returning to Bombay on a Monday morning. The train was to have two sets of carriages with restaurant cars for first- and second-class passengers.

McKay had his work cut out at Matunga as the coaches had to be ready for their inaugural run on 1 June 1930. He worked hard and worked his workers hard. He picked up phrases in Hindustani from them and over the years became quite fluent in the language. As he got used to Bombay and its climate, he discarded the suits and waistcoats of colonial uniform and dressed in simple sleeveless shirts and baggy workmen's trousers.

He lived during those years in the bungalows set aside for railway sahibs in an enclave called Vile Parle a few miles south of the yards. He lived as bachelors of the Raj did, dining at the Railway Club or commissioning his servants to provide what he wanted.

Every few weeks he would go to the shipping office at the docks and pick up letters written to him and deliver letters to be sent to Scotland. He told his colleagues that he didn't trust the Indian post, and his communications were important enough to be entrusted to the personal care of couriers whose acquaintance he had made and whom he could approach for the favour.

The other engineers who had arrived with McKay to supervise the setting up of the new trains returned in due course to Blighty, but for reasons he didn't explain to these colleagues, McKay petitioned his company to stay on in India. He delineated the several ways in which he could be useful to the company and its railway enterprise in India and they, short of experts who would be willing to come out to the colonies, readily agreed to his request.

Soon after the colleagues who had come out to India with him left, the servants of his household were burdened with the care and commands of a memsahib. She came off a steamer with very scant luggage, and she and Mr McKay were married in a ceremony in St Anselm's church. No invitations had been issued as no guests were invited.

*

My first glimpse of Stuart McKay was at the gates of our school in Poona. Two khaki-clad peons, the porters and general dogsbodies on the school's servant staff, were holding him at the gates and refusing him entrance. He was dressed in faded baggy blue cotton trousers and a dirty brown shirt with a blue handkerchief tied round his neck. His blonde hair was uncombed and unkempt. He had holes in his shoes. He was an unusual sight in our town: a white, or as my grandmother would have said, "a European" tramp, a fallen sahib.

A teacher went to the gate to negotiate with him, and a crowd of pupils gathered just within the compound at the sound of the altercation. McKay was shouting. He wanted to see his boys.

The teacher turned to the crowd of pupils and told us to go away and to get to the "lowers", the playgrounds behind the scattered school buildings, so-called because they were situated down a slope in the volcanic soil behind the tennis courts.

There was a reluctant move a few yards away from the gate, but this crowd wasn't going anywhere. The drama was too promising to miss. We were hoping the white tramp would put up some physical resistance and we'd see our teacher assaulted. This teacher, one who had no reputation for severity or even for authority, sent one of the peons to fetch help. It certainly looked to us now as though McKay was threatening physical force to pass the teacher and the peons and wander into the playground.

"Oi, *chhokras*, tell my boys Pater is here to see them," he shouted at the crowd of spectating pupils.

He didn't say who his boys were, but one or two of the seniors knew whom he meant and went winging off to find Golly, Jamie and Doug Mckay.

"Kalu!" someone who had spotted our headmaster shouted, and the crowd of pupils began to trot away from the gates.

Mr Appleby, the headmaster, a small, squat and dark-skinned "Anglo-Indian", an authoritative and brilliant teacher, with a deputy in tow, both of them wearing their black gowns over their tweed jackets, approached. Kalu, "blackie", was the rude name successive generations of pupils knew him by. The teacher at the gate renewed his efforts to tell McKay to go away, feigning a renewed enthusiasm for the task, but McKay had spotted the approaching Mr Appleby and knew where authority lay.

It was only later that the peon who had remained at the gate to bar McKay's way told the senior boys to whom he sold contraband cigarettes and from whose mouths the rumours spread, that the headmaster had confronted McKay, told him he was drunk and that the police would be summoned without compunction, whereupon McKay had started to weep and said he only wanted to see his boys. At the gate if necessary.

"You want money from them, don't you?" the deputy had asked him.

"I love them," McKay said just as Golly, Jamie and Doug, alerted about the scene at the gate, ran up.

Mr Appleby in wisdom and compassion said they could speak to their father at the gate, but they were not to give him any money, however much he pleaded. Then the head turned the other teachers and the peon away, and they walked a little distance to give the boys and their derelict father their open-air privacy.

Golly used to sit at a corner desk on the last row in our classroom. He wasn't a bright pupil but that wasn't through a lack of intelligence. He didn't care for any of the learning that was imparted in lessons. He copied his maths homework from me and when challenged to answer questions in class, was prompted in whispers by his neighbours who fed him keywords of the answers under their breath. He got by on occasion with these.

He was a good sportsman but even on the hockey field or the cricket pitch he gave the impression that he was trying to preserve his energies for something beyond the sport, giving the game and team the least effort he could get away with.

He was called Golly because he had frizzed out his blonde hair when he first came to the school and though he was a white-skinned Scot, he acquired the nickname and then adopted it. His hair was now cropped short and was far from curly but the name stuck. He signed himself R.G. McKay. He looked after his younger brothers and they looked up to him. We also knew that the school maintained the three boys through the Anglican church's Orphans' Fund.

The fund paid their board and lodge, and the headmaster and a few of the other teachers subsidized their upkeep. The charitable donation wasn't sufficient to give the three boys a bed and place in one of the school's dormitories, so they had beds in a crowded makeshift room on the side veranda of the headmaster's house, which stood in the centre of the school's vast compound.

Some of the other buildings of the school were old army barracks converted into classrooms, dormitories or teachers' quarters. Mr Appleby's boast at each parents' evening or open day was: "Don't come to us to see our bricks and mortar. Come to us and see our boys!"

Golly was something of an amateur sculptor. He would get blocks of wood and using a couple of sharp penknives carve animals and human figurines out of them. He spent a lot of time in the classroom carving his bits of wood and the plastic handles of toothbrushes under the desk, barely pretending to pay attention to the lesson.

I had two points of special connection with him. On the days when we had to hand in our algebra or geometry homework in the morning before the first bell, I would, being a day scholar, cycle a half-hour early to school and hand over my maths exercise book to Golly who would copy the sums and proofs to the geometric riders, which I was reputed to always get right.

For a few weeks he had acquired a reputation for being mathematically astute, until the teacher quizzed him on a geometrical proof he had copied from my book and deduced the truth. Golly was caned in front of the class for lying and cheating, and I was similarly thrashed for abetting his deceit. It made a bond.

Golly used the bond. In our penultimate year at school, when I was thirteen and he was a couple of years senior, he fell in love with a girl in the all-girls' school across town that my sister attended. Golly commissioned me to pass his love letters to my sister to convey them to the girl and bring back via the same link, her replies. In return for my couriering service Golly carved me a devil out of a black toothbrush handle and pierced a hole through the devil's feet so I could thread it on to my key chain. It was a proud trophy.

It ended in tears. About two weeks before his pater called at the gate, Golly was summoned to the headmaster's office. The passing of notes had been discovered by the headmistress of the girls' school and one of her notes, filled with forbidden allusions and sexual fantasies, had been intercepted. Golly didn't tell me what the headmaster had said to him, but I too was summoned and told that I had been an agent of wickedness. I would be spared a beating this time, but I was not to carry any notes to anyone in the future. I was asked to say I was sorry and to write a note to the headmistress of the inamorata's school to apologize for burdening my sister with the duties of a carrier of immoral messages.

Golly, however, was disgraced and punished at an assembly of the senior school where he had to present himself on stage with a cardboard plaque around his neck that said "ROTTEN ROMEO".

Mr Appleby lectured the senior school. "Parents send their children to boarding school in the hope and the certainty that they will be looked after as they would at home and will not be allowed to drift into bad company or bad ways. Think of your sisters and cousins being sent to such a school. Would you like them to be enticed into some disgusting tryst with some boy from another school?"

And so it went on till Golly was asked to take his punishment like a man and was publicly given three strokes of the cane. He came to class swearing revenge under his breath.

The day after their pater visited, I was summoned to Golly's room. He wanted to apologize for the embarrassment he had caused me by asking me to be the conveyor of notes. He said the time had come for retribution. He said he had made some lemonade from the limes and sugar he'd stolen from the Appleby kitchen, and he brandished the jug and poured me some.

He mentioned his father's visit and wanted to know if I had seen him. I said I'd caught a glimpse.

"He used to be a brilliant railway designer and he didn't want to go back to England when the other sahibs left, so we got stuck here."

I indicated that I and the rest of the school knew that.

"But look what's happened to that bastard. He wanted cash of course and Dougy gave him two rupees. I told him not to, because Pater will just go and buy more of Uncle Frankie's hooch with it and fall in the gutter. When the police pick him up they treat him well because he's a white man and some of them know he was a sahib in the old days."

"Where does he live?"

"In Bombay with his black whore," Golly said. "I don't know her and I don't want to know her. I've never seen his slum. Jamie has. He knows the whore and calls her stepmother. That's why Dougy and I don't speak to the bastard."

The whole school was aware that there was this rift in the McKay family between Jamie and Golly. Till then I didn't know why. Jamie was a favourite of Mrs Appleby, the head's wife, and as a reward for running into town on errands for her, she would buy him new shoes and invite him to dine at her table when the head was not there. I had assumed that Golly and Dougy resented this favouritism and that was the cause of the tension between them. This was the first time Golly had actually told me what the base of the difference was.

Most of the senior school knew that the McKays were dependent on the school's and the Mission's charity. The brothers knew and I suppose we knew that their mother, a Scotswoman, had died a few years after giving birth to Dougy.

"But you must like him a bit at least. He's your father."

"I hate him. He's a drunkard, and he picked up that Indian whore. He kept her in Bombay while we all lived in Poona. That killed my mother when she found out."

"How did it kill her?" I asked.

"I don't really know, man. One day I'll get it out of the son of a bitch. Maybe she just died of a broken heart. My nightmare is..." He broke off and paused. "What I really don't want to be told is that she killed herself and left us with him."

We were sitting on his narrow bed. He didn't want to think about it anymore. He jumped up and pulled out a battered metal trunk from under the bed. He seemed to have put thoughts of his mother and the encounter with his pater away.

"Will you be at scouts tomorrow?"

"Of course," I said.

"I want to see Kalu's face. He's in for a shock," Golly said. He was grinning.

I didn't know what he meant.

"Still got some work to do," he said mysteriously. "How many badges have you won?"

"I got my Pathfinder's and the Cook's. That's all," I said. "I failed the First Aid because Appleby asked me what I would do if someone had a snakebite and had fainted and I said I'd call a doctor."

"You have to suck at the snakebite, pull the blood and poison into your mouth and then spit it out," Golly said with real authority. "I can give you the First Aid badge if you want. Forget what Kalu says."

He opened the metal trunk, which was full of scouting equipment, the various badges members of our scout troop could earn, with which he had been entrusted in an attempt to give him some responsibility and keep him out of mischief.

"No thanks. I'm reading up on First Aid and will tell Kalu that I'm ready for the test. I'll get it this time."

"Mug," he said. "I'll see you tomorrow."

We assembled the next day. Golly was my patrol leader and as such had to stand at the head of his seven-scout patrol. We took our positions as Mr Appleby and Mr De Lane, our two scoutmasters, came up in their uniform and blew the whistle to indicate that we should "fall-in". There was an air of anticipation under the spreading banyan tree where the school's 1st Poona Troop assembled each Saturday in term time.

"At–ten–tion," and there was a clicking of heels.

"Stand at ease!" and the stomp of forty-two feet.

Then they spotted him.

Golly had stitched on his khaki sleeves and down the whole front of his shirt one each of every category of scout badge from his trunk. His shirt was covered with the coloured embroidered badges of every skill a scout could master and be certified for.

"McKay, what are you wearing?" Mr Appleby thundered.

"It's my uniform, man. And red and white striped *chuddis* under my shorts, but you can't see those," Golly replied in a perfectly unexcited matter-of-fact tone.

"You get that off," Mr Appleby shouted.

He was furious. The explosion we had anticipated when Golly turned up was threatening to roll over us.

"You come and get it off me, Kalu ... or try," Golly said.

Mr Appleby and Mr De Lane lunged forward. Appleby had a scoutmaster's staff in his hand. He lifted it menacingly, but Golly was off.

"Whhhooooo ... aaaa..." the cry went up from the scout troop.

One of the best runners in the school, Golly ran fifty yards towards the right-hand gate and out of it on the road from where, across the low school wall, he grinned at Mr Appleby.

"You come back here, McKay," Mr Appleby said.

Then Golly took his shirt off and flung it across the school wall at Mr Appleby.

"You want your shirt, you wear it, Kalu. It's yours, isn't it? Everything I am wearing is yours, isn't it? But not my flesh and blood. We are not yet slaves, Kalu."

Mr Appleby had stopped in his tracks. Golly was crying.

The comedy vanished.

"You come back here," Mr De Lane said, walking out of the gate and on to the road towards Golly.

Golly didn't move. De Lane walked up to him and put his hand on his bare shoulder.

"Come on, lad, let's get you inside," he said.

Mr Appleby walked away to his house. He didn't want to face the scout troop who had hooted and jeered as he forgot his dignity and chased Golly. Mr De Lane, accompanying Golly into captivity or to his rooms, shouted to us.

"Troop dismissed for the day!"

We scattered. I saw Golly shaking Mr De Lane's hand off his shoulder. Bare to the waist, he sat down on the steps of the headmaster's house. De Lane had some words with him and then walked off. The other scouts observed this, but no one approached Golly.

I did.

"You okay?"

He started laughing and coughing as he laughed, holding his head in his hands, tears filling his blue eyes. I didn't know whether he was laughing or crying.

"It was worth it just to see Kalu's face," he said.

"We all saw it. I've never seen him lose control like that," I said. "What do you think he'll do now?"

"Beat me in public, I suppose. I don't care. I'll take my medicine like a man. That's what that bastard my father used to tell us. It's not as though we're not used to beatings. Except Jamie. He was the darling. He's gone off to see Pater and stepmummy by train to Bombay. Mrs Kalu paid for the weekend trip. Bitch."

I didn't know what to say.

"Golly, how did your dad, if he was a designer or engineer or whatever, get to, you know, being without a job?"

"The fucker thought he'd stay behind and become head of the railways or something. But you know what? He talks like a street *chhokra* boy, all the filthy abuse in Hindi and all, but he used to kick his employees and call them names. He'd call his Indian officer 'you black buck!' and stuff like that."

"Like we call Kalu?"

"That's a joke. We love Mr Appleby so we tease him. Pater used to hate the Indians who worked for him and called them Sambo and all this. Then as soon as the management changed from Brits to Indians, the top man called him in, and guess who it was—the Indian guy who'd been his assistant. He told Pater that he was transferring him to some job he didn't want in the stores or something so Pater told him to fuck off and tried to assault him. So he got thrown out of the service. By which time he was with his whore, and he started drinking and smoking Indian hemp and all this—stuff his whore had taught him. That was the end man."

"That's a sad way to go, man," I said.

"You know what Pater, the dirty swine, calls his black whore?"

He was sombre now, and he nodded to himself as though calculating something in his head. Then he looked up at me.

"He calls her his Deccan Queen!"

*

(Miriam—nothing to add to this chapter except that a school friend called me out of the blue and said it was accurate, and he recognized all the people even though I had changed their names on your advice, and he even said he remembered the incidents I have outlined.)

Yerawda

Two rivers meet in the heart of Pune: the Moola and Mootha, and at their confluence, their *sangam*, are two bridges, one for road traffic and the other for the railways over which twice a day the Deccan Queen rumbles to and from Mumbai. Beyond the confluence, the river, now unimaginatively known as the Moola-Mootha, flows past a garden built on a high bank. Below this bank, which one descends to the water on stone steps, the British administration of the town built, of the native black volcanic rock, a bund, a small dam, over which the top layers of the water flow to make a less voluminous river downstream. The park enclosed and cultivated above the bund is known as Bund Garden, and there we were taken as children by our ayah to play with the other children till sunset.

An image stays with me from those days. Perhaps my first intimation of death. A man had brought a bundle on a bicycle in which were five or six newborn puppies. A crowd gathered to watch him bind their legs with string and take them down the stone steps to the river to drown them. Our ayah kept us away from the execution, but there was a great deal of noise from the curious crowd, above which I remember the squealing of the pups. Each time I pass Bund Garden my heart sinks with the memory.

Beyond the bund and the garden runs the unimaginatively and obviously named Bund-garden bridge. Both banks of the river now boast fully fledged development and miles of internal city. In the days when I was at school and college the right bank of the river held the town and the left bank—as one faced downstream—was known as the suburb of Yerawda. The name was a corruption of *yed vadda,* Marathi for "lunatic asylum", the prison-like stone building situated a few hundred yards from the bridge.

The suburb also boasted a little hillock called Parnakooty with an industrialist's white house on top, visible for miles around. The house used to host Mahatma Gandhi as a guest when he visited the town then called Poona.

Further along the river from the bridge, going upstream past Parnakooty was Poona's famous Deccan College, a collection of grim stone buildings, converted British army barracks, but a citadel of learning in the nineteenth and early twentieth centuries. Going downstream there was the fortress of Yerawda jail, notorious as the place of execution by hanging of felons convicted of murder.

Still further down the river on the "suburban" bank of the river was the palace of the religious leader the Aga Khan. When Mahatma Gandhi was arrested by the Raj for political agitation he was kept under house arrest in this stately home. I suppose the Raj thought that felons high and low belonged on the west bank.

*

The new history teacher in our school was an Indian Christian called Bal John. He was a wiry young man with deep-set eyes and a complexion darker than Kalu's. He had been appointed after the death of Mr Williams, one of the old teachers who filled the gaps in the teaching curriculum by taking classes at all levels in anything from handicraft to French.

The school held a memorial for old Mr Williams and we sang:

"As pants the Hart
For cooling streams
When heated in the chase
So longs my soul
Oh Lord for thee
And thy refreshing Grace."

It was, the headmaster announced, Mr William's favourite hymn. I always wondered about the words. I didn't know that a hart was a deer and thought it was a misspelling in our hymnbook. And I could only think of "pants" as a noun. I am sure the rest of the school pupil congregation were just as perplexed, but we sang it heartily in memory of old, mild, puzzled Mr Williams.

We thought Bal John's name strange when he first appeared. He was in every way the opposite of Mr Williams. He was, as he claimed himself, "an intellectual". We hadn't heard the word before. He was a PhD in history and had studied the history of the Indian railways for his thesis. He was intolerant and a snob and was very rude to those who didn't follow or absorb his lessons which were, unlike what we were used to, lectures on selected subjects from the syllabus.

Bal John appeared in our penultimate year in school and was, for me at least, a refreshing change from all the other teachers. He was a rebel of sorts. He would openly criticize the procedures and disciplines of the school and was contemptuous of the low intellectual standards it had set itself.

"This school is letting you all down. You can be scholars, but all that this staff seem to care about is football and sports day. I'm going to change all that. There's no bloody respect for scholarship in this place. The boxers are more important than the mathematicians."

I had never been called a "mathematician" before, but he pointed to me because I had the best marks in geometry in the class.

The rumour in the school was that he was an atheist, and he was openly contemptuous of assemblies and religious observance and had argued with the headmaster and the senior members of staff over disciplinary procedures.

I and a group of what Bal termed "the budding intellectuals" would gather in his room long after school, and he'd make us tea and buy us buns. He called it his "circle", and we would discuss the politics of the day. He would read extracts from the newspapers and encourage us to debate the issues thrown up. Will the law against taking, giving or asking for dowry have any effect? Should India go begging to Russia to give us some aid to build the next hydroelectric project? My classmates and I hadn't encountered any such stimulation from anyone, and it felt then like a new way of being.

The only non-intellectual that Bal John was interested in was Golly McKay. He turned to me in the circle one day and said he knew that I was close to Golly.

"As close as any of the others," I said.

"You carried notes for him to some girl didn't you?" Bal said. "And Kalu whipped both of you for something or other." He used the derogatory nickname the headmaster had acquired in the presence of his circle.

"It wasn't Mr Appleby, it was the maths teacher. He beat us because I let Golly copy my homework."

We appreciated the fact that he exposed himself to our trust by using the headmaster's derogatory nickname. He assured us that very many members of staff referred to him thus out of his hearing.

"But call him. Tell him he's welcome here," Bal said.

I told Golly that he should come along one evening and at least eat the currant buns that Mr John routinely supplied at our confabs.

"I can't talk all that history and politics and stuff man. And John said he hated boxers anyway, so what's he calling me into your little brain-hurting crowd for?"

But Golly did respond to the invitation, and after his second appearance in the circle it became evident what Bal John was after.

"Your father," he asked Golly, "does he ever talk about how the Deccan Queen began? He was there, I believe."

"I don't talk to him," Golly said. "But in the old days, when I was very young, he talked about nothing but the bloody railways."

"That would be so interesting. I'd love to talk to him," Bal said.

"You got the wrong McKay, sir. You want my brother Jamie who still sees the old man. Me and Dougy don't and don't want to."

Bal got the message. Golly understood that he had only been invited into the circle so Mr John could access some memory of his father's about railways. Though the invitation was not withdrawn, Golly never came back. It wasn't his natural habitat, this hothouse of discussion and debate in the two small rooms at the end of the junior dormitories that Bal John was supposed to patrol in return for the accommodation.

Bal did precisely what Golly had indicated he should. He was seen on several occasions talking to Jamie McKay on his own. Jamie was my age but two academic years down. Bal didn't teach those classes, but he asked that Jamie be transferred and put under his care as a senior prefect of the junior dormitory of forty boys in his charge.

One weekend Bal and Jamie took leave and left school. Golly deduced and told me that they were going to Bombay. The silence between Golly and Jamie was broken when he returned.

Golly was away from classes the next day. I went after school to his veranda, but none of the McKays were there. The next day Golly was back in class, sitting silently in his corner at the back and, we assumed, carving his wood or plastic under the desk as the geography teacher went through the natural causes and vicissitudes of the monsoon's behaviour.

My desk was in the second row from the front. I was half listening to the master telling us why the heaviest rain fell in the northeast in Cherrapunji, but my mind was on Golly. I instinctively felt he was too silent, much too turned into himself.

I rose from my desk. In our senior years we weren't challenged for that sort of thing. I went to where Golly sat. He had been carving under the desk, but it wasn't wood or plastic he had cut into. It was his wrists. The blood pulsed from them onto the floor. He looked up at me, his eyes pools of liquid in which his blue pupils swam. His head fell to his desk. I remembered my scout First Aid and the drill for tying tourniquets. I took my tie off and tied it around one of his biceps. The geography lesson continued for a few seconds till the teacher noticed what I was doing.

"What are you doing there?"

"He's slit his wrists, sir," I replied.

The class rushed to where we were. Six boys dragged and carried Golly out of the classroom and to Mr De Lane's car. He was driven to the hospital.

Golly returned in two days. He had lost blood and been given sedatives and blood transfusions.

Mr John didn't take the history lessons the next day. Rumour spread that he had been called to Mr Appleby's office, and a loud and dreadful shouting match had ensued. They could be heard all over the playground. Bal John emerged from the head's office. He had been suspended.

Golly, his wrists bandaged, was brought back to his room. Jamie and Dougy were hugging him when I left my classroom and went to see him. They were all crying.

"She's not dead. She's alive," Golly said to me.

"Who?"

"Mummy," Dougy said. "She's in the madhouse. She didn't know who we were. She's chained up." Then he began to howl as though he was in pain.

Jamie shed silent tears.

"How do you know?" I asked.

"Mr John found out and took us to the mental asylum. They treat them like animals. I didn't recognize her, but she was the only white woman there. She was dressed in rags and tied up. We tried to say we were her sons, but she didn't know anything. It was like she didn't see us," Jamie said. "She could see, man, her eyes were awake, but she was blind, like what she saw wasn't connecting to her brain."

Jamie turned to me. "Golly said, 'Mummy, I am Richard' ten times, louder and louder, till the guards or whoever they are came and told him to shut up. He was crying, 'I am Richard,

Mummy, I am Richard' but she didn't hear or make sense of what was going on."

"I'm going to kill him," Golly said. "I don't care what happens to me. I'm going to kill him and his black bitch, his Deccan Queen."

A Song

I must have been four years old. My mother and father would dance to the music of the wind-up gramophone. One of the records they played and danced to was called "Cheek to Cheek". Its lyrics went:

I'm in heaven
I'm in heaven
And my heart beats so that I can hardly speak...

That was when I was four years old.

Then, when I was forty and living and working in London, my mother, by then widowed, came from India to live with me for a few months.

One lazy evening she was watching TV, and a drama featured this particular song. She sang along, and of course we—myself, my partner and friends who happened to be there—accepted that it was a song from an era that must have brought back memories. It did for me, and my mother remarked on the very thing it brought back.

"It was very strange," she said. "I remember clearly dancing with Daddy to this song, you know, just in our sitting room to this record on the gramophone, and we would imitate the actors we had seen in the cinema and dance close, cheek-to-cheek, and you were only four years old, but you used to get very jealous and tug at my sari and tell us to stop. You didn't want me dancing to that song with Daddy at all. Daddy thought it was very funny that you were so possessive and teased you by continuing to dance cheek-to-cheek."

"All these years you thought I was tugging at your sari because I was jealous?"

"If a four-year-old can be jealous," she said.

The company was amused.

"No, Mum, thirty-six years later I can tell you, I remember the song and you dancing with Dad as clearly as though it was yesterday, and it had nothing to do with jealousy or your dancing cheek-to-cheek with Daddy. It was the song. I had somehow picked up the idea that you only went to heaven after you were dead, and when you sang 'I'm in heaven' I thought it meant you were dead or accepting of death and that terrified me. That's why I tugged at your sari and told you to stop."

"Oh my God. That never occurred to us," Mum said.

Asperogers

My uncle Khurshed, younger brother of four sisters of whom my mother was the eldest, worked in Bombay as an engineer, and now that he was earning his own living and could even send a small amount home each month to supplement his father's pension, declared that he wanted to get married. He wasn't asking for the traditional search for a suitable girl to be initiated, he said. He had already found the girl he wanted to marry and insisted that he was deeply in love with her.

I was about eight years old at the time and my mother's family—her mother had died a few months before—lived in Poona. A family conference was called that evening as my uncle, in his late twenties or early thirties, was impatient to seal the deal and get the families together. He looked upon the conferences and examinations as a formality.

My grandfather, who always stood a bit aloof from matters of birth, marriage, death and most other things, entrusted the talks and possible arrangement to my mother Shireen, his eldest whom he regarded, after the death of his wife, as the senior lady of the family.

The four sisters gathered to hear their younger brother out. He confessed that he had already proposed to the young lady.

"She is younger than you, isn't she?"

"Not too much younger? No cradle-snatching?"

"Have you seen her birth certificate?"

"She's not pregnant already, is she?" my youngest aunt, Amy, wanted to know. She was a few years older than Khurshed and the closest to him in childhood as they were the babies of the household. Amy isn't a Parsi name; my grandparents' fourth child had been named by her elder sisters who happened to be reading Louisa May Alcott's *Little Women* from which they had plucked the name.

"Well, is she?" Amy asked again.

Khurshed frowned and shook his head as though he and Amy were still children, and he was warning her off that sort of talk in front of their seniors.

"Don't talk nonsense," my mother said.

"Does she have a family? Where do they live?"

He had already told them that her name was Freny, and they knew her surname, which they muttered and repeated like a mantra as though a familiar family tree would manifest itself out of the air.

"No, never heard the name before," my eldest aunt said.

They asked my granddad, who was attending to his vast stamp collection, dipping paper hinges in a bowl of water and sticking specimens that had been sent to him in a bundle into one of his thick leather-covered albums. He said he'd heard the name but didn't know anyone who answered to it.

"Of course she's got a family. A mum and a brother who's just got married. Her father died ten years ago."

"And where do they live?"

Khurshed was a bit reluctant to divulge their address but knew he had to.

"A few streets away from my flat," he said.

"That's a slum," Amy said. "Last time I stayed in Bombay I had to wade through garbage coming and going from your front door, and you should put a proper bulb on the staircase."

"Whereabouts?" my quiet aunt Shera asked.

"It's Khetwadi. It's a Parsi colony. Not far from where our own *masi* lives," he said, alluding to my grandmother's older sister.

"Parsi charity houses?" two of them said.

"I didn't say she was rich. She works as a secretary. Her father's dead, and they are living off what she and the brother earn," he said.

"Rich, poor, we don't care," my mother said, in a chairwoman's tone. "And we are not snobbish about them living in a Parsi colony."

That was the word universally used in western India for groups of buildings that rich Parsi philanthropists, some of whom had amassed fortunes in the opium trade to China, had built for the poorer families of the community. These buildings with four or six flats each, with twenty or fifty such buildings to a compound, were dotted around the whole of Bombay, and with a tight-knit community such as the Parsi Zoroastrians of India, one was bound to know many of the families. Any Parsi family tree would have some poor branch with a "colony" address.

That evening we cousins were each given a rupee by Khurshed as extra pocket-money—Bombay largesse and a fortune to each of us.

It being the hot season, we slept on the veranda on mattresses on the floor, and the collection of cousins discussed the matter in hand.

"Mamu wants to get married to his girlfriend."

"Then there'll be new cousins," the youngest amongst us said.

"That's only when they sleep in the same bed. That's how cousins are born," said my sister.

"Of course not. Lots of people sleep in the same bed, look at the six of us, we are not going to wake up with babies, are we? It's the priest who says secret words and puts babies in the stomach of mummies. They can only say the secret words when they are marrying someone and have been paid already. My aunty told me," our eldest girl cousin said. It seemed a decisive opinion.

A group of gas-lamp carriers heading for a wedding procession somewhere in the city cast a chiaroscuro of moving shadows of pillars, posts, the shapes of the bougainvillea bush, the wrought-iron trellis of the neighbours' veranda and the shadows of passers-by on the wall opposite where we slept. The distraction of this "cinema" ended the discussion.

Two days after the family confab, my mum and my eldest aunt, Mani, the married one (named after the third-century Zoroastrian heretic who divided the world into good and evil and gave rise to Manichaeism), travelled to Bombay on the Deccan Queen to check out the family of the young woman who would, with their approval, become the prospective bride and would have her relatives visit us in Poona on a reciprocal family-approval mission. We woke up early to see them off before we bathed and changed into our school uniforms.

They spent four days in Bombay and returned, without Khurshed, in time for the weekend family gathering. Everyone was eager to hear their report.

I wasn't, at the age of eight, invited into the conference, but we children were just as curious as the rest and found ways of hanging around and eavesdropping.

"She's pretty, very nice, well-mannered, not terribly well read—she didn't know who Jane Austen was," my mother said.

"I don't know who Jane Austen is. I don't watch too many American films," my uncle Dorab, always called Dolly, said.

"The nineteenth-century writer," my mother said severely.

"How would I know? I don't read Shakespeare's novels!" Dolly said.

The conference should now have been persuaded that a familiarity with English literature was not a necessary criterion for marrying into this family.

"And her family?"

"The mother is what you'd expect—an old-fashioned Parsi lady still wearing a widow's dark sari in the old-fashioned style. Doesn't speak English…"

"Neither could Mamma," Amy said.

"Yes, but she could bargain with the egg-seller in Marathi and with the fish-monger in Hindi," my aunt Shera said.

"So do we approve?" Dolly asked.

"Yes, I think we do. And Khurshed really likes her so…" My mother shrugged. "I'll tell Pappa."

"So where did you meet them?"

"We were invited to their house for dinner the first night. And they'd gone to a lot of trouble," my aunt Mani said. "I think they'd bought new crockery just for us because the paper label with the price was still stuck on the bottom of my plate."

"That was very sweet," my mum said. "And of course they all said that Freny had cooked the meal, all of it, all by herself. It was a feast. Very good *dhan daar* and Bombay Duck and *bhida par eeda*."

"And this brother and his wife?"

"They live in the same flat, so they were there for dinner," my mum said, smiling and frowning at the same time. "Bit of a strange fellow because all through dinner he had this unopened can of asparagus with him, and he kept picking it up from the table and thrusting it towards us for our attention and saying 'Asperogers, asperogers!' He seemed very proud of it."

"Did he open the tin?"

"I thought he might, but he'd just brought it to the table to show us."

Later that night, when my mother was reading to us before bed I asked her what asperogers was.

"It's called asparagus, a kind of vegetable, a sprout, which is imported. You wouldn't have seen it, it's green and knuckly, but I don't think it grows anywhere in India."

"Then why was the brother showing you the tin? Is he a fool?"

"You shouldn't have been listening to the grown-ups' talk," Mum said.

"But if he's a fool, why are we letting Khurshed Mamu marry his sister?"

"Of course he's not a fool, darling. He's very clever. He works in a bank. He just likes Khurshed and wanted to show us that he knows about and eats foreign delicacies, and I suppose wanted us to think that it was quite expensive. He was trying to impress us, bless him. He must have got it specially from one of those smugglers who sell you foreign junk on Grant Road."

Smugglers! In school we had recited a poem about smugglers and had to learn it by heart. When my mother turned out the light and left us to sleep on the veranda, I remembered it, and the rhyme went round in my head.

Four and twenty ponies
Riding through the dark
Brandy for the parson
'Baccy for the Clerk
Laces for a lady
And letters for a spy…

And asperogers for the man in Bombay who wanted his sister married into the right family.

Falling asleep I watched the wall with its rapidly moving shadows as the headlights of cars went by.

*

(Miriam, a letter from Canada disputing my account—perfect for what you wanted for the Second Edition. – fd)

Toronto,
Canada

Dear Mr Dhondy,

Having read a review of your recent book I took the trouble to order and buy it online.

I was aware that I was distantly related to you through the fact that you were the uncle of my mother's cousin—but I am told that all Parsis can find such connections if they keep at it and allow their family-trees to spread like the Indian banyan, sprouting roots out of branches. I was proud of the fact because I too want to be a writer and am taking a semester in creative writing at my Canadian School. No longer.

I think you are scum. You misuse the medium of prose and of the past recollected in tranquillity when you write about my grandfather in a callous and abusive way in the "story" or section which you entitle "Asperogers".

Yes, that gentle, gentle man was my grandfather—my mother's dad and one of the most affectionate and caring people I have ever known.

Albeit, I only knew him when we visited Bombay—or Mumbai as we must learn to call it—when I was five and six and then eleven and fourteen. The last time we went was to attend his funeral, a sad and even, for us Canadian Parsis, a curious if grim affair at the Towers of Silence.

I've read some of your earlier books and always thought of you, at least as a writer, as moderately sensitive. But here you were abusing my grandfather, poking fun at him, basing a whole episode of your not-too-engaging book on his mispronunciation of the word "asparagus". Yes, so Indians and others do mispronounce words but the attitude of your family to this small mistake of a kind man was, to say the least, snobbish and callous.

Did your mother and her sister not have the grace to look beyond a vegetable can? Did they not understand his enthusiasm and possibly even gratitude towards the young man who had made an approach to be his brother-in-law?

I did meet your uncle and of course my grandaunt and they were very hospitable. My mother's cousins are still in touch and one of them has indeed migrated to Canada as my mother and father did soon after they were married.

My sister who is a lawyer says we can't sue you because you can't be held for libelling the dead—and my grandfather is dead.

Perhaps you can reply to this with a tiny heartfelt apology for the hurt you have caused my mother and my family? Or is that beyond those who choose to call writing their profession? Does all heartlessness go with the job?

Repent!

Your reluctant "relative",
Naju Watchmaker

★

London

Dear Naju,

I am pleased to hear you have abandoned the ambition to be a writer and given up on the creative writing course.

I am pleased because you've probably saved time to get on with other things instead of wasting it on creative writing courses.

Your complaint about my account involving your grandfather indicates that you shouldn't be a writer. You don't have the insensitivity for it.

I wish you the best in whatever else you choose to do.

Ever,
Farrukh Dhondy

The Poona Intercollegiate Zoroastrian Association

My father had returned from the Second World War, from the Andaman Islands, which the Japanese had occupied and which British-Indian forces had retaken. He was full of anecdotes about the landings, fierce fighting, the victory of the infantry brigade and the capture of Japanese officers who surrendered their swords, a few of which he had brought back as trophies.

I was fascinated by the swords, but being two or three years old when these stories were told and retold to family and friends, I could make nothing of them. The war, I was told years later, was what had kept Daddy away at my birth. I didn't note his absence at the time or in the months following. One doesn't.

There was, however, a name from one of his tales, mostly whispered and told and speculated about in very sombre tones, that made an impression and stayed with me. It was the name of someone my father and mother had known. It was, I gathered, through several years of my boyhood, the most important story of my father's war years and of his recollections. I pieced it together when I was about twelve years old.

The name I remembered from the eavesdropping, because it was a story that was not for children, was Jingo Mama. It remained with me because the name Jingo was unusual and the surname was the same as the word in Gujarati or Hindi or most Indian languages used as the respectful title for one's mother's brother. As a surname it struck me even then as absurd. It was as though an Englishman were called Ziggy Uncle.

*

My mother, born Shireen Antia, went to Dastur school, which had been founded and endowed by rich Parsis of Poona. Most of the Parsi Zoroastrian children of the town went to that school, which was at the time run by English women.

Their headmistress was a grand lady called Miss Amery.

Shireen's fast friend at the time was Mani Noble, another Parsi girl from a family that lived not far away from the Antia household and neighbourhood.

As Shireen and Mani reached the graduation class of the school, they became, by virtue of their proficiency at studies and by the relatively mature, if still mischievous personalities they had formed as a consequence of looking after their young siblings and other juniors, the teachers' favourites. Miss Amery was very fond of them and very ambitious for them.

Most Parsi—and most Indian—girls of their generation finished school and stayed at home till suitable matches could be found for them. They would traditionally learn to cook and sew and have some instruction in the arts of housekeeping in a joint family and how to be good daughters-in-law, and then the wider family would be alerted to the need and consequent quest for a suitable boy.

Shireen and Mani wanted none of that. They wanted to go to college and were actively encouraged by Miss Amery and other teachers in this ambition. In the weeks after they passed their final exams, they would go to the school and help out as teachers' assistants, occasionally taking classes and generally making themselves useful. These were the weeks in which they had to apply for places at college, and they both proposed such a course to their fathers.

My grandfather and Mr Aspandiar Noble, Mani's father, were having none of it. Girls didn't go to college, especially Parsi girls. They attempted to point out to their fathers that at least one Parsi girl, one Jeroo Dastur, a girl from a rich and socially leading Parsi family, had completed two years in Nowrosjee Wadia College, an institution of Poona University endowed by a leading Parsi family.

It didn't convince either Ardeshir Antia or Mr Noble. "Our girls don't do that" was the attitude, and they dutifully and sadly reported this to Miss Amery.

One sleepy and hot afternoon, a British horse carriage drove on to the streets of our neighbourhood and stopped. Undoubtedly carriages of that sort, carrying British personages, did pass, if infrequently, through the neighbourhood, but it wasn't the sort of locality that would occasion a visit from an English lady.

This one had business there. Miss Amery stepped out of the carriage and called, without notice, on my extremely astounded grandfather. Of course she was invited in, and Shireen and my grandmother were put to dusting off the best crockery, preparing tea and sending as fast as possible to the bakery on East Street for cakes and biscuits.

Miss Amery got to the point. Shireen had to go to college and study for a degree. It would do credit to the family and the community and would be the waste of a talent if she didn't. Besides, she would not be alone because Miss Amery was next going to call on Mr Noble and attempt to persuade him to send Mani to college too.

My grandfather was, according to my grandmother and my mum, quite transformed. He became, over this cup of tea and biscuits, a staunch convert to the further education of Parsi girls in general, and of course if Miss Amery was in favour of Shireen going to college he felt compelled to agree. Miss Amery naturally quoted the example of Jeroo Dastur who had passed through the school and had with her family's blessings enlisted and was well on the way to being a graduate.

Miss Amery followed up the victory with a visit to the Noble household and they, having been forewarned of her visit by my young uncle being sent as a runner with news of the certainty of the surprise, had prepared the crockery and tea with cakes and biscuits by the time she got there.

It was done. Both fathers had agreed to allow their girls to enrol, and my mother and Mani Noble were to join the degree courses after the university holidays in three months' time.

Then circumstance overtook. The Parsi community of Poona was scandalized by the elopement of Miss Jeroo Dastur with a Mr Dehlavi, a Muslim young man from her college.

It was Romeo and Juliet to the young but Capulet and Montague to the outraged community. The pair had fled to his family in another city, and poor Jeroo was, at least by the community and perhaps just for a time, cast into disfavour.

That was it. My grandfather and Mr Noble aborted their consent. Shireen and Mani would stay home and learn to cook and sew at their mothers' and grandmothers' knees. The suitable boy agenda would be revived. If Parsi girls who went to college ran away with Muslim boys and brought shame on their families and communities, no persuasion could shake the revised resolve.

It could be mitigated though. Miss Amery called again. She brought another grand English lady, the principal of the Poona Teachers' Training College, with her. The neighbourhood was again abuzz with curiosity. Not one, but two English ladies had entered the Antia household. They had come to persuade Ardeshir Antia to consider allowing Shireen to attend the Training College where boys and girls were strictly separated for all leisure activities and even for most instructional classes.

And so it was that my mum joined the Intercollegiate Parsi Society of Poona, of which my father-to-be Jamshed Dhondy was the male secretary for that year. Mani Noble had been elected lady secretary at the same time. My dad was a Bombay boy and so was one Jingo Mama, and they had both enrolled in the Poona Engineering College and subsequently in the Poona Zoroastrian Collegiate Association at the same time. While they knew each other, they weren't fast friends in Bombay, but in the small collegiate community, sharing rooms in Poona Engineering College and studying for their degrees together, they became fast and reputedly inseparable friends.

My mother's Training College was part of the university but seen as second best to the degree-conferring colleges, for which she had been destined and which Jeroo Dastur's dereliction or romantic choice and the play of prejudice had deprived her of.

Nevertheless, the Parsi Intercollegiate Association met often enough for Shireen and Jamshed 'Jimmy' Dhondy to share each other's company, go to the cinema and for picnics and cycling and walking and no doubt sneak off on their own to go dancing and to do it cheek-to-cheek and in short, to fall in love and resolve when they concluded their studies and when Jimmy was earning a living, to get publicly engaged and married.

Very few of their friends knew of their serious intent, but Jingo Mama and Mani Noble said they'd keep it a secret. There might have been at some point before their relationship bloomed an interest from Jimmy in Mani and an interest from Jingo in Shireen and perhaps even vice versa, but this never resulted in any mid-monsoon night's dream, confusion or jealousy. It remained a vague possibility banished to the road-not-taken or to "what-if?" land. The phase, which must have existed because it was referred to later, even by Mani's son and myself who, when we were adult friends, speculated on the fact that we could, but for the grace of providence, have been brothers, passed, and it was Shireen and Jimmy who made the secret tryst.

Neither family had done things that way. The generation before them had very strictly supervised, traditional, arranged marriages in which love, if it came, came later. Love before marriage would have been considered by Ardeshir H. Antia and probably by Khurshedji Dhondy, my dad's father, as carts before horses, a formula for going nowhere.

Both Shireen and Jimmy were the eldest children in their respective families, so the question of the way one got married had not yet been tackled in their generation.

They graduated and celebrated with whiskies, beers and shandies at the Zoroastrian Intercollegiate Association, which held these graduations at the Poona Parsee Gymkhana. Jimmy went to Bombay to look for a job, and Shireen enlisted with the friends she had made, three Parsi girls she had met in college, as teachers of infants in St Helena's school, a Protestant mission school whose girl-pupils wore bright green uniforms and were teased in town as "the *totas*", the parakeets.

They wrote to each other, and Jimmy, after a few engagements as a civil engineer in out-of-town building projects for Parsi master-building firms, decided to follow what he took to be Mahatma Gandhi's call and enlisted in the officer corps of the British-Indian army.

Now that he had secure employment and was assigned to a proud regiment, he made bold to approach an aunt of his and take her into his confidence. Could she broach the subject of his finding a suitable girl with his parents and would she connive to say that she knew of one such from a very respectable family in Poona.

His aunt's highest recommendation for any girl and one that was a guarantee of her virtue and virginity was that the girl was "innocent *ney* ignorant", the two indispensable qualities. This aunt didn't speak many English words beyond these, but they were high praise.

At first my grandparents and my father's other relatives fell for it and dispatched the very same aunt and another senior relative to negotiate on the family's behalf with the Antia family of Poona, taking the tentative proposal of a liaison with her if the girl, on being viewed and examined, was deemed suitable. My grandfather Ardeshir H. was not deceived for a moment. He spotted the set-up by his daughter and the young man whom he had seen in the house a few times; the engineer-fellow whom his daughter had casually mentioned was now an army officer.

The proposal went well. The horoscopes matched, and the only hitch was a comparison of birth certificates. The girl was a few days older than the boy. The conference of relatives from both sides would have seen this as a serious impediment, but both the conniving aunt and Ardeshir H. exposed the plot.

"Look," he said, "this is none of anyone's business. These young people know each other well and have for three years.

They are both intelligent and educated and they want to get married and they must know that my daughter is a few days older than the boy. No harm can come of that. I am very glad that they have both gone about it the right way by involving the consent of the families and so if you have come all the way on the Deccan Queen and have to catch that train back tomorrow, I can say I and my lady wife here give our consent. We know the boy, he's from a good family, he has a profession, he is now an officer in the army so no more of this charade."

He was not normally one for speeches, but Conniving Aunt joined in and the compact was sealed.

Jimmy came on a visit wearing his army uniform. Jingo Mama had enlisted at the same time and was assigned to an artillery regiment. He had rediscovered his childhood sweetheart on his return to Bombay and was now engaged to her.

It was 1938 when they enlisted, and the talk in Europe was of war. In 1939 Britain declared war on Germany, and the Empire was alerted and declared to be a combatant. Both couples decided to prolong the engagements as Jimmy's and Jingo's regiments were transferred to military bases in remote parts of India. They each had to seek permission to marry from the colonels of their regiments, and this permission was forthcoming, but they were both advised to delay getting married till the army in India was certain as to what it was doing.

It was two years before my parents got married.

On 7 March 1942, the Japanese invaded and captured Rangoon, and as the British army retreated, the British-Indian army was mobilized for the fight back. My father's honeymoon leave was cancelled, and he rejoined his regiment. My father's and Jingo Mama's regiments were both ordered to the front. My father said he was eventually sent to the Andaman Islands and when those were secured, moved north through the Burmese delta to the interior. Jingo's regiment was part of the army that retaliated against Japanese-occupied Burma through Assam.

The battalion to which his regiment belonged suffered heavy defeats and casualties, and the Japanese captured thousands of British-Indian soldiers and held them in prisoner of war camps where a campaign of propaganda, beginning with the officers, began to convert them to the cause of defeating British imperialism.

The ex-Indian National Congressman Subhash Chandra Bose sided with the Germans and Japanese in the war and called on soldiers in the British-Indian forces to desert and join his Indian National Army, which would, with the victory of the Japanese, expel the British from India and win freedom from colonial rule. The Japanese were not looking to replace the British as an imperial power; they were friends and allies of the freedom struggle, and their now proven military prowess would help India get rid of the yoke of British imperialism.

The Indians in the Japanese POW camps were barracked with this message day and night, and when their officers converted and preached to the troops who had been in their command about the virtue of changing sides and pledging to fight with the Japanese, many soldiers accepted and were recruited to the Indian National Army. My father very honestly admitted that he didn't know what he would have done if the Japanese had taken him prisoner of war.

The "nationalist" army, this INA, never fought any serious battles. It was doubtful whether the Japanese, who immediately afforded them better treatment and the status of watched-over allies rather than enemy prisoners, would ever allow or trust this army in serious battle. Could the turncoats or born-again patriots be trusted to fight and kill the countrymen and comrades with whom they had fought side-by-side and with whom they had shared rations and shortages and danger weeks or even days before?

Jingo Mama was one of the converts. He had, so Jimmy reported when he got back from the war, gone over to the traitors' army, fought for the Japanese in a skirmish south of Kohima and been killed in action.

The story of his dereliction and death were confirmed in a British government's posthumous court-martial report, which was sent to Captain Mama's widow. The British-Indian government was in a dilemma at the end of the war when the Japanese had been forced to retreat and then surrender. What would they do with the defectors from their own army ranks to the INA whom they had subsequently captured? Should they be asked to publicly recant? Should they be put on trial as traitors? The Indian national movement was ambivalent about these men. Were they martyrs or misguided patriots? Were they traitors and fascists assisting the Japanese to impose a far more repressive regime than the British had ever done? What would be the fate of India if it were recolonized from the East by the new world empire of the Axis powers?

There was a general feeling that those who had gone over to the Japanese-supporting INA had done it to end the misery they suffered in the POW camps. Some confessed that they had never intended to fight for the Japanese against their former comrades. Some said they had followed their officers. Those officers who didn't recant and defiantly stood behind the late Subhash Chandra Bose, who had died in a plane crash over China, were put on trial as traitors.

Jingo escaped all that. He was dead, his body left to rot somewhere in a jungle in northern Burma as the Japanese were forced into a slow and later precipitous and ignoble retreat. He had left behind a widow and a child, still a babe in arms, who had never known his father. Jimmy and Shireen attended the funeral prayers in Bombay, which Jingo's family organized for the peace of his soul.

I heard the story of Jingo Mama's defection and death a few times in my childhood. I overheard it incidentally before I was of the age to enquire into the currents of the Indian national movement and before I could debate the issues and politics around the personality and stance of Subhash Chandra Bose.

I must have been eleven, a good eleven years after the war, when my father was posted to Kanpur, formerly Cawnpore. My sister and I spent our school holidays with my parents, and that summer I was in their bungalow in Kanpur playing by myself in the garden, digging a ditch and trying to make bricks out of mud and straw. I was going to bake them and build a dog kennel.

It was a large garden in which our army cantonment colonial bungalow was set. The house had a porch in which my father parked his maroon Mercury. In front of the porch was a large circular lawn on which there were several cane chairs and a cane table at which on Sundays my father and perhaps some of his friends would have a beer. It was a large enough garden for two gardeners to work at it under my mother's supervision and large enough for me to have carved out a corner for my, largely unsuccessful, digging and building experiments.

It must have been late afternoon when I heard a gentle call from the gates, which were shut against the possibility of intruding cows and goats that had been known to invade and eat the flowers. I looked up and saw two figures clad neck to toe in saffron robes with near-bald heads.

"Young boy," the older one said.

I left my pit, shaking the mud off my hands, and went to the gate. One of the monks was perhaps in his forties, though telling the age of adults was not something I could do, and the other much younger. They had cloth bags hung across their chests, and they each carried a wooden bowl.

I approached them. They were obviously not begging.

"Is your father at home?" the older one asked.

"He's at the office," I said.

I could now see that his face bore a scar from his forehead right down to his neck and perhaps further into his saffron garment. I also noticed that he clutched his wooden bowl with one finger and his thumb and that the other fingers of his right hand were missing. There was also something about his left eye that was not right. I stared at it. It must have been the first time I had seen a glass eye, but I immediately knew that it was.

"Is your mother home?" he asked in English.

"She's inside," I said.

"Can I speak to her? Will you call her please?"

I didn't know whether to invite them past the gate, so I decided to let someone else take that decision and turned and ran to the house to fetch my mum. I told her that there were two monks asking for her.

"Monks? For me? What do they want?"

She came out of the house and walked across the lawn to the gate, and the old monk smiled, even though his brow was wrinkled at the same time. My mother stopped several yards from the gate. She held her hand to her mouth. No words came for perhaps half a minute.

"Hello, Shireen," the older monk said.

My mother shook her head.

"No!" she said. "No, please."

"Can we come in? Is Jimmy back soon?"

"No, tell me … I mean he is, he should be, but how…"

She unlatched the gate, which they could easily have done, and stared wide-eyed at the monk.

He stared back.

"No, I am not dead," he said. "You are over the shock, I think."

"It can't be," she said. "Come in, come in. How ... where ... Jingo. He should be back any minute."

She was indicating that they should enter the house when they followed her.

"We can't come in. We shall sit here if that's permitted," Jingo said.

"Yes, yes, sit here," Mum said. "What can I get you to drink? Where have you come from? Why..."

There were too many questions, and they went through the threshold of utterance and fell away. He answered the simplest one.

"We'll have some water," he said.

Mum looked at me, and I ran in and fetched two glasses of water.

They had settled into the cane chairs on the lawn by the time I returned with the water. I didn't hear what he said to Mum, but when I came back with the water she was sitting with the two monks and the pallor and shock had receded from her face.

"This is a beautiful garden," the older monk was saying.

The younger one hadn't uttered a word.

Then my father's car came to the gate. His horn blew, and one of the gardeners appeared from nowhere to open it. Dad swung round the drive, parked in the porch and, tapping his thigh with his military swagger stick, strolled across to greet whoever was on the lawn with Mum. The two monks got to their feet to greet him, and Mum took a few steps forward, saying nothing. I was sitting at a little distance on the grass, and I didn't stand up. I was unaware of the nature of the mystery that was unfolding before me.

Dad stared at the older monk and dismissed the idea that he recognized him.

"Hello, good evening," he said and joined his hands in what he must have taken for a pious greeting. Then he stared at the old monk again.

"Hello, Jimmy," Jingo said.

Dad looked at Mum as though to ask what sort of trick this was.

"It's Jingo," she said. "He wasn't killed in Burma."

"Oh my God," Dad said in a whisper.

"It's good to see you settled and happy, and I met your son," Jingo said.

"Where…" Dad couldn't get the words out.

"Let's sit down and I'll tell you. When I enquired around Kanpur and heard your name, I thought I'd make contact. You are the first people from the past I've been in touch with since my return."

"You mean Ratan doesn't know?" Mum asked.

"She's happily married again," Jingo said. "How can I disturb that? I can only bless her. I am a monk."

"Take these," Dad said to me, holding out his officer's hat and swagger stick, "and tell Gaffur to bring us tea."

I was reluctant to leave but of course had to do what Dad said.

I returned and sat unnoticed on the grass behind Dad so he couldn't see and send me away. I knew that some intriguing story was to unfold.

Jingo said he was captured late in the war in 1943 at a place called Jessami in Manipur. His artillery company, commanded by a British officer, surrendered to the Japanese. The Indian officers, himself included, were willing to fight to the end rather than surrender, but the odds were heavy, their supply lines had been cut and they had lost communication for days with the rest of their regiment and the battalion. They surrendered to the Japanese who shot the British officers and took the Indian troops captive.

Three senior Indian officers, who had, he assumed, been previously captured by the Japanese, now wearing Indian National Army colours and bearing their former officer's ranks, were sent to their POW camp to speak to the recently imprisoned officers. They talked very convincingly about the inevitability of a Japanese victory, about the Bengal famine that the British had imposed as punishment on the Indian population, about the British using Indian troops and civilians as cannon fodder, about the Americans having a plan to use Indians as slave labour with the connivance of the Raj, about how the Japanese Emperor Hirohito had pledged himself to the freedom from European domination of all Asian nations and of how we would as the Indian National Army march triumphantly to great acclaim from the population into Delhi.

It was, Jingo said, convincing stuff, and it came from senior officers whose reputations as patriots could not be questioned. Yes, he signed up. The prison regime was relaxed, and he was asked to speak to his jawans, the troops he had led who were now prisoners of war. He failed to convince them after two or three lectures to which the troops squatting before him listened in silence. They began to sing "Vande Mataram" even as he spoke, and his Japanese handlers knew he had failed in the task of conversion and swept him off that platform and sent him back to the INA convert camp.

The Japanese in charge of them moved them from Jessami to a place called Ukhrul over very rough terrain. They said it was a fresh offensive, but it seemed very much like a retreat through the jungles. The British and Indians were all around them. He said he couldn't recall how or when but he was hit by a shell and had half his face torn off and several pieces of metal pierce his body. He had fifteen scars all over, and he was blind in one eye. He may have been left for dead had not an INA jawan, one of those who had switched allegiance, dragged his still-breathing body back to the position to which the Japanese had retreated.

This jawan later told him that the Japanese commander didn't want to demonstrate to the other INA men and officers that they would leave a wounded INA soldier to die, so he was given the best medical or nursing attention that the retreating army could spare, and he found himself, when he regained consciousness, on a hospital ship that had left Rangoon to try and get in a final retreat to Japan. He must have spent more than a year in hospital and lost count of the number of times he was taken to the operation theatre to remove metal from his body, to remove the smashed eye, to lobotomize part of his brain, to amputate his smashed fingers, staple with metal wire the bones of his jaw and through all that and several blood transfusions to keep him alive. What plastic surgery was available at the time was later applied to his face and neck.

The Japanese doctors, nurses and administrators whom he had encountered befriended him and made themselves understood by patiently teaching him Japanese.

"I left the hospital, and the Japanese army gave me a small pension to live on. Of course I thought of returning to India especially as Japan was overrun with American troops, but I was warned that India was putting what it called traitors and defectors on trial and they may, even a year and more after the war had ended, put me on trial, imprison or execute me. Things seemed to move very rapidly. There was of course talk of independence for India and it happened amazingly fast. All of you must have celebrated for days!"

"I was in Naushera trying to prevent the slaughter at Partition, and Shireen had to bring the children back to India from Quetta, where we were stationed, on an army train," Dad said. "But why didn't you come back after Independence? All the INA boys were treated as heroes at that time. Remember Prem Saigal and his cronies?"

"The other INA officers who had defected with me were not sure that I was a firm believer. The fact is I was not. I would have been treated by both sides as a traitor. I may have been. I don't know. But by then I was living with one of the Japanese nurses who had looked after me, and she found work for me translating Japanese menus and instructions in road traffic code books and even Christmas cards into English for the American influx. She only spoke three words of English—she'd say 'I love you'. I hadn't mastered Japanese, but I would falteringly, painstakingly find out through her what the written Japanese meant. I was in a daze. And then, Jimmy, Shireen, there was the fact of starting and being stuck in a completely different life. I don't know if anyone ever has the strange experience of being convinced that they are someone else.

"I tried to imagine people with amnesia who had been transported to where no one knew them having to start over again. It was like that for me, and though there was a terror in it, there was also a challenge and a feeling of being a child at the age of thirty, having to discover and adjust to a new world. I shouldn't say challenge. It was a sort of momentum of inertia if that makes any sense—I know we are both engineers and that's not good mechanics, but it's the best way I can put it."

"I can understand that," Mum said and cleared her throat.

"You must recall that I was the joker of the pack in the Parsi Association, and all that was gone. Nothing in the world was funny. That way of looking at things had dissolved in the pain that wouldn't leave me night and day. I was given medications of all sorts, doctor's medicines and herbal devices. My brain hurt, my body was racked with pain all over, I couldn't even say where, and then a friend of my Japanese partner took me to the Zen clinic, and they taught me ways of meditation. It was a kind of yoga but combining mind and body exercises.

"It's what I did for months day and night, and the pain began to go, but with it I found myself transformed with a new discipline. I began to eat and drink only that which I strictly needed, and my body didn't want sex any more. Hanako, my lady partner, understood, though it made her sad. It was a sort of parting of beliefs. I was detaching myself from all bodily and material wants, and she believed that body, mind and spirit had to be brought into a balance so as to make the most of life, love and the earth.

"I knew I couldn't live with her any longer and asked the Zen ashram that had cured me and put me on the path if I could join them. The chief monk, after a few months of instruction in the ways of the order, called me and said I should go back to India and find myself there. It was plain to him, he said, that I was making a start there which would not be fulfilling. Japan is too enclosed for you is what he said.

"I took his advice and landed in Bombay. I wasn't dressed as a monk. The first thing I did, Jimmy, was go to your house in Byculla. I hesitated before knocking on your door, and then couldn't find the courage to do it. I turned back and asked your neighbours in the gully who was there and was told you were in the army and never there.

"It took me two weeks of living in cheap hotels to convince myself that I should go and find Ratan and my old home, and like some prospective thief I waited on the pavement outside for hours till I saw her emerge with a boy who I knew was my son by calculating his age. She was pushing a pram. She had a new baby."

"Yes, she married again when we all thought you were dead. She waited for years. She was officially told that you were dead," Mum said.

"Someone you know, actually," Dad said.

"I wish them, from a distance, all happiness," he said.

"So you didn't approach her or let her know?"

"No. What would be the purpose of that? I wandered for a few weeks and then went north by train to the Himalayas where I had heard of this order of monks, Buddhist Gnyanis, the origins of the philosophies and disciplines of Zen. And so here I am. It's so good to see you both."

"You'll have to give me some time to recover, *dikra*," Dad said. "I haven't got over the shock."

"There should be no shock," Jingo said. "The world performs and we are entitled to wonder."

"How is it that you are in Kanpur?" Mum asked.

"We are walking along the Ganga from its source to Benares," he said. "We eat whatever we are given in our begging bowls and live in the open on the journey, though we are quite modern. We each have haversacks with our spare clothes and prayer beads and things, which we have left outside your gate. We didn't want you to think we were attached to baggage!"

He smiled.

"Are you hungry? Shall I order a meal?" Mum said.

"You must eat something," Dad said.

The young monk looked at Jingo.

"If you have some fruit, we'll take it," Jingo said. "We can't accept your hospitality and sit at your table. Forbidden." I clearly saw him wink.

Mum went and brought a whole basket full of fruit from the dining room. Jingo and the young monk filled their bowls with oranges, guavas and bananas.

"There's anything you want, bread, biscuits," Mum said.

They both shook their heads and thanked her.

"We should get going, Shireen, Jimmy. But that's the story. For you."

The monks stood up and now Dad noticed me and asked what I was doing there. I scampered off and saw Mum and Dad escort them to the front gate.

That night when Mum came to turn the lights out in our bedroom I asked her if she was going to tell Jingo's wife.

"No," she said. "If he wants to come back from the dead, he has to do it himself. Now go to sleep."

*

(WOW! The most important reaction for the Second Edition. – fd)

From: Brigkarunk@gmail.com
To: fdhondy@lucidwriting.co.uk

Dear Farrukh,

I am the young disciple who came to your bungalow gates in Kanpur more than fifty years ago with the person that you in your novel have called (the reverend) Jingo. I should say really I was that young disciple, because I am no longer young and no longer a disciple in my body but only and always in my heart.

I am making the assumption that you were the young boy who let us inside the gates and then summoned your respected mother who then offered us seats on her lawn and entertained us till your respected father arrived in his car.

I must tell you that though I said nothing at the time and probably was not even conscious at the time of thinking anything that strong, it was your father's entrance that had a profound effect on me. You see, all my young days I had been brought up, first by the family that I don't clearly remember and never owned in this life and then by the monastery to which as an orphan I was sent by distant relatives, to believe that life follows a discipline. I had even at that young age seen many lives derailed by indiscipline and having no goal. Yes, I had naturally moved from one thing to another in my life without choosing it. There was no conscious choice in becoming the disciple of whom you call (the reverend) Jingo—who by the way is no more! He passed to his next life eight years ago in the monastery.

I was given the begging bowl and knew it was my destiny to follow where he led and to beg for him and keep first his and then my body from falling into hunger and thirst leading to weakness and dysfunction. I repeat there was no choice. I was like a drop of water in a stream going with the current.

It was when I saw your father with his military stick and hat and uniform that I realized here was a person who had put on the garbs of order through choice. I knew that the reverend Jingo had also been in the armed forces in a previous life—without a previous birth, mind you—and that he too must have made a choice to give up that and to join our order and monastery as a monk.

It took me four years to realize it, wandering the world with the reverend Lama. Four whole years of begging and sleeping by Himalayan streams and then I made my choice. I would leave this life of the monasteries and of the open sky and the winds and enlist in the army where a life of discipline would lead to self-realization. It would be a life of my choice and the Great Sakhya Munni himself said that choice is all we have to regulate our karma.

My karma led me into the Indian army—in fact through the agency of your father whom the reverend Jingo made contact with when I expressed my wishes, and it was your respected father who wrote a letter on my behalf to the recruiting agency in Ambala. I joined as a Junior Commissioned Officer and I would like to tell you my adventures.

I was soon transferred by my seniors to the Intelligence Corps, and it was destiny that three years into the service I took my army uniform off and had to don the robes I had willingly discarded and go in the guise of a Buddhist monk again to the shrines in Pakistan Sind as one of the delegates whom the Pakistani government would allow across the border through the agency of the American influence which was then leaning on the Pakistan government to allow visits to the Buddhist shrines of Sind of which there are many.

My mission, about which after all these years I can say very little, was to gather information from Indian agents within the Pakistani borders of Sind and bring it back, which is what I did.

Again, my dear Farrukh, I cannot speak of the dangers I encountered on this mission but I can tell you that I wasn't playing the part of a spy when I was a lama again because I knew how to be a lama. I did not stand out from the delegation at all, marching stiffly while my other Buddhist brothers shuffled in their gait as do the monastery dwellers, or took wild long steps as some lamas do, being used to walking for hundreds of miles.

I finished my career as a brigadier in the infantry and retired some years ago. I have now returned to my native Ashom and live here on my own. My monkish life never taught me how to be emotional with women or even be attracted to them so I was never married.

Now you may be thinking why is he after all these years writing to me. Let me be quite honest. If you would consent, I want to send you the autobiography of myself which I have been composing since my retirement. It is called *The Monk Who Soldiered On*. I hope you will agree to read it and promote it with your publishers.

I'll tell you the exciting thing about my book, which is full of all sorts of coincidences and twists and turns of fate. You being an author and a well-read person must have read the books of Rudyard Kipling and must be familiar with his masterpiece *The Adventures of Kim*. Now in this book, the young boy Kim and his friend the Tibetan Lama—who came from a monastery not far from where I was brought up—set off to Ambala where they meet a person in charge of British

Intelligence, an officer called Colonel Creighton. That is just one coincidence that I started my spy career at the same place. Or shall we count that as two? One about the monastery and then the town from which it all began? Two beginnings!

Which I have pointed out in my manuscript.

Then you will remember that in Mr Kipling's novel the lama has lost his young disciple. This is what happened to (the reverend) Jingo who lost me when I took another path.

The lama of Mr Kipling was looking for the river of life that would lead him and so was I, and I found it in the army and in military service to my country and my faith. Remember that the fundamentalist Muslims of Pakistan and Afghanistan where *The Adventures of Kim* is partially set have now destroyed all the Buddhist shrines, and the statues of the Great One at Bhumiyan have been dynamited in vandal destruction.

I might tell you, sir, that when I was brought up in the monastery there were no statues of the Bodhisatva allowed. We used symbols like footprints to signify that we would follow in his path. It was when I came to India and then Pakistan that I saw these magnificent representations of Our Lord. So, many things about the quest and life and fulfilment are the same in my book and that of Mr Kipling and you might find these interesting.

You will see from the book that several things you have said about the life and adventures of (the reverend) Jingo—several things which are not accurate. I do not mean by this to insult or blame you and very much hope that you will not bear me a grudge for knowing the story more intimately and in a fair and frank manner contradicting some of the facts in your book. You will see that on page 103 of the manuscript I mention you in passing and for six pages onwards from there talk about your respected mother and kind father.

Even you put in an appearance as the boy at the gate. (I had written these pages before I came across your book and so did not mention your name but if you insist I can change that and say "now he is a famous author").

So I hope for old times' sake you will assist in this way.

If you ever think of coming to Ashom please e-mail me as I shall be eagerly awaiting to have you as my guest on this humble tea plantation that I have been fortunate enough to acquire in retirement.

Your friend,
KK
Brigadier (Retd.)

PS You can also write to me at my organization at:
Monkwhosoldieredon@gmail.com

Plus Ça Change

My neighbour, Pervez, a precocious boy of fourteen who was, we suspected, a particular and intimate friend of Father Simeon, a French Jesuit priest at his school, had cultivated the habit of exclaiming in French.

"*Mon Dieu,*" he said one day. "The Deccan Queen track is being made new and then it will get to Bombay in less than three hours."

He had read about it in the national newspapers, which no one else of our age bothered with.

"There is going to be a penicillin factory built in Pimpri," he announced. "That's why they are speeding up the links between the hinterland and the coast. *Plus ça change.*"

The French phrases and the use of words such as "hinterland" with which he spiced his pronouncements gave him a certain authority. Otherwise he was a figure of ridicule. It was Father Simeon who bought him a new pair of spectacles after he roamed around with one lens missing, substituted for by a patch of black paper stuck into the plastic frame with sticky tape. He insisted it was his weaker eye and didn't hamper his vision. We knew he was too proud to admit to his family's poverty. His father worked for the Municipal Corporation driving a refuse truck, which carried away stinking waste and offal from the meat and vegetable markets.

The grey truck, which he sometimes shamelessly parked in the streets of our neighbourhood, gave off a rank smell. The girls of the neighbourhood whispered amongst themselves that the smell clung to Pervez, which is why they called him "perfumez".

He was a loner. When the rest of us teenagers of the neighbourhood strutted around Main Street, went to the cinema or hung around the street corners in the evenings after school and after the football and hockey we were compelled to play, he would spend his evenings somewhere in the cloisters of his Jesuit school's staff quarters and retreats.

"We listen to French records. You won't have heard of Debussy, your head is full of Billy Haley and the Comets. *Quel dommage*!" he would say as we chatted sometimes across the partition that separated the railings of the front verandas of our side-by-side houses.

He was right of course. My head and heart were full of the music and the influence of America that burst through the radio and the films that were our window into the pulsating rocking and rolling world.

But dear reader, the story is best told by Pervez in circumstances that will become clear:

*

Je suis Pervez. *Cette un nom Persian et ancien*. I want to blame no one and am writing this so that the world will know the truth about human feelings and about its own hypocrisy. I have read the great books. I have even read *Madame Bovary* in French (I don't mean to boast so I will add…) with the help of a translation. Is it not clear to any reader of that great work that there is no such thing as sin, but only human weakness, desire, disappointment and tragedy? Father Simeon explained to me what the great book really meant, and he thought it was a very Christian novel, even though a lot of people have said it was the devil's work itself.

How may I pretend to be Emma Bovary? I am not and never could be, being born an Indian Parsi, but the heart of two people, separated by history and geography, by time and culture, can still beat the same. Someone reading this to the end may conclude that I have got the wrong character, the wrong sex, that men and women can never feel the same things, but I have cried when reading Emma's story, and I have looked into the well of her despair and seen my reflection in the surface of the deep waters there.

I would say that Father Simeon and I were friends. Anyone who understands the nature of deep friendship will not question this. The word can mean so many different things, but Father Sim and I understood what it meant to share our thoughts, my process of growth in his shadow, or in the palm of his hand—where he treated me with such gentle severity.

For my part, Father, I thought you had the only grasp that a human being has ever had over events, the world, the spirit, people, history and reality. I am convinced that no one else I can ever know commands the truths of the world as you do. You once told me that a young girl would fall in love with me only if I could make her believe that I held the secret of all futures in me—her future, the future of society. "These girls fall for those who can make them believe they will possess the world, my boy."

I knew he was testing me. About girls. I told him I didn't want a girl to fall in love with me. What I didn't tell him was that I felt about him exactly as that imaginary girl felt about the person she was falling in love with. I know he knew it. He knew how I felt. Actions spoke so much louder than words and yes, Father Simeon, you were not hesitant with your actions. Or I with mine.

It was bliss. The companions of my neighbourhood and my classmates and schoolmates couldn't understand our connection. Father Simeon (he knows all this, but I write it for the unfamiliar reader) would come to my classroom and ask the Brother's permission to take me out of class because he trusted me with tasks he could not hand to any other boy in school. The envious loafers would hoot and whistle each time I was summoned, shouting, "*Wyey, wyey*, chic chic chikney..." and any other rudeness that filtered through their ignorant spongy brains to their mouths.

Father Sim would set me tasks like fetching the homework books of a junior class or tidying up the physics cupboard—which of course couldn't be done by the illiterate servants—and sometimes even profound things like adding up the attendance registers of the whole school and helping him make a statistic with the figures.

After school we listened to records in his rooms—French records, and he would read books to me. What we had in common was a love of engineering because before he took holy orders he had trained in Belgium as an engineer. He admired and loved great feats of building—roads, bridges, tunnels and railways—and he always said that one of the reasons he had chosen Poona as his mission station was because it was the capital of the Deccan and the British had built the magnificent rail link to the cities of the coastal plain. He meant Bombay.

He also loved engines, the steam ones and then the electric and diesel ones, and it was he who explained to me the difference between an internal and external combustion engine. He said that though the world thought James Watt and George Stephenson worked out the theory and built the first steam engine, it was really the invention of a French engineer, a Christian La Salle Brother, but he had allowed his invention to be stolen because of his natural humility.

Three times we went on Father Simeon's motorcycle to spend a night or two in Khandala, living in a hotel where they didn't know or care that he was a priest or a white man travelling with a younger Parsi boy. We would spend the day walking along the tracks descending the ghats and climbing them again, and he would point out to me the features of the excavation of tunnels. He would explain how the mountainside had been levelled to make the roadway for the railway line, and we would watch the engines and their trains pass by.

Of course I couldn't tell Daddy and Mummy that I was going alone with Father Simeon on these excursions. A few weeks before the trips I would pretend that I was off to a scout camp and would be away for the night or two nights of the weekend. Daddy never suspected anything, though the way my mother asked questions about what we would eat and whether there'd be enough blankets in my bedding roll to keep me from catching a cold made me feel guilty and nervous.

I secretly took my Agfa box-camera with me. I say secretly because Mummy and my sisters would have been very curious to see the range of boy scouts at the camp, and of course there would be no boy scouts. There would just be photographs of railway lines taken from the tops of tunnels, of escarpments and of impossible twists in the road and of the trains, including the Deccan Queen, flashing by. And of course there was the photograph I was most proud of, taken from below, of Father Simeon standing on the famous rock called the Duke's Nose.

Father Sim taught me when we returned (after our first "honeymoon" as I called it), how to develop and print the film. I kept the photographs pressed in the pages of my chemistry text, which I knew the family wouldn't venture to open.

The Duke's Nose was the big black protrusion that Father Simeon insisted was known amongst the British railway workers as the Jew's Nose. However, the sahibs of the Survey of India department, not wishing to offend their Jewish colleagues, had changed it to offending some mythical duke instead. I always told him it should be called the Parsi's Nose now that the kings and dukes have departed. I said he should see my uncles and my aunts and he would know what I was talking about. He thought it was a good joke.

Getting to the Duke's Nose took us three attempts. The first time we had to turn back in the jungle as we had set out in the morning and by late afternoon we knew it would still take us several hours of fighting through the underbrush to get to it, and then we would be in the dark. Father Simeon looked at the detailed maps he had in order to find another route to it, and this time we took camping equipment on our backs and approached it from a village on the ghats far from the Bombay–Poona road on the other side of Khandala.

We got to it the same evening because we started early, and then we camped and pitched the light tent by a waterfall where we washed our faces and drank. Monkeys attacked the tent at night, and we shone torches to drive them away. It was the next morning that I waited while Father Sim climbed the rock. I snapped the picture of him looking like he had conquered Mount Everest, and then he shouted down to me to scamper up the smooth protrusion that hung over what Father Simeon said was very fertile volcanic soil, down thousands of feet to the coastal plain.

It was after that glorious trip that Vasco came into our lives. He was an orphan sent and paid for by the cardinal in Bombay. Being an orphan, he was given a bed in the dormitory in the school, and for some reason he attached himself to Father Simeon.

He was a small but handsome boy with dark but clean-cut features and he didn't have, as I have, a bit of a hook nose.

He was good at studies, and soon I couldn't help but notice that Father Simeon was giving him the little tasks around the school that at one time he may have given me.

Then Vasco began to attend the sessions we used to have in Father Simeon's room where we would eat cake mixed and baked in the school kitchens with recipes that Father Simeon invented and listen to the French records and talk about books and railway engines.

I shouldn't even say he started attending these sessions. The truth is he was always there in Father Simeon's quarters. When I was invited round and went home after school to return on my bike to the residences behind the school facing the football grounds, he would be there fiddling with chess pieces or sketching. Mostly sketching. He was good with the pencil and great with the paints, and in the first two months that he was there, he did one pencil drawing and one painting in watercolours of Father Simeon.

Of course I was jealous. I could see that Father Simeon was trying to be careful to show me that our friendship had not been interrupted by the arrival of Vasco. It may have changed in certain ways, there may not be as much exclusive time for me or any for that matter, but still nothing had qualitatively changed.

How could he deceive himself? Everything had changed. I would hang on till late in the rooms with him and Vasco, as late as I could manage, knowing in my heart that the two of them wanted me to go because Vasco had to return to the dormitory by curfew, and they were wishing and praying that I would volunteer to leave and go back home so they could have their moments together. Was it just my imagination?

Daddy would ask me what I was doing out late, and I would tell him I was having individual French lessons with Father Simeon, and I would show him the exercise books I carried. Daddy couldn't really read English, leave aside French. He had given up the driving job and was now a trader in the poultry markets, so the one luxury we had was chicken for dinner three times a week, when other families could only afford it on birthdays and at Christmas.

Yes, cycling home at nine o'clock, leaving Vasco in Father Simeon's rooms always left the thin saliva, a sort of venom of disappointment, flowing from under my tongue. My mother would berate me for not being home in time for dinner, though she would offer me what she had put aside. I would sleep without eating or at least go to bed and toss and turn till the early hours when after a brief sleep I would have to get up and bathe from the hot bucket and get my uniform on and walk to school. Vasco always seemed fresh on these mornings and would greet me cheerfully.

I was plagued by the idea that I couldn't compete. This ability of his to paint was the devil. Father Simeon got the other Jesuits interested in Vasco's painting talents, and he was set up with an easel and a broad canvas in the quadrangle of our school to get what Father Simeon called "a visionary view of St Anselm's".

I watched the panorama on canvas coming on day after day. It was a realistic angled perspective of the courtyard and the stone-walled quadrangle with the fountain and the statue of Mother Mary and the infant Jesus to one side. The attention to detail was fascinating; the cracks in the paint of the window frames of the first- and second-floor classrooms reproduced exactly as they were. Father Simeon pointed these out to me in his rooms, to which the canvas was returned when Vasco was not working on it. The painting was to be sent to the cardinal, Vasco's patron and guardian, when it was complete.

"I thought, Father, you always said that the day of the realistic painting with all this attention to bloody detail was dead because of the invention of the camera," I said.

He knew I was annoyed.

"There's no need to swear, Pervez. And that was not all that I said."

"Yes, you did. When you showed me Picasso's work and Matisse and I said that nothing looked real, you said that all that was over because civilization didn't need that sort of real painting anymore and that the vision, the poetry of God's creations, whether the human form or landscapes or bowls of flowers, was what the modern artist was trying to capture."

"Yes, I said all those things, but that doesn't mean that representative art has no place in our world. And anyway, look at the painting. It's not precisely like a photograph, is it? The light and the shade come from Vasco's vision. What he sees."

The words that crossed my mind were "damn his vision and damn his eyes and damn your hypocritical adjustment just because you want to flatter the boy and suck up to the cardinal by showing him what a brilliant thing you have done with the orphan he sent you". I said none of it.

"You don't look happy, Pervez. Would it help if I told you that I am planning one of our little trips to Khandala? You, me and Vasco, and you can show him the Parsi's Nose. Maybe he should do a portrait of you in silhouette standing against the background of the rock." He laughed.

I wasn't going to be a spoilsport. I laughed too.

"We can take Vasco's canvases and paints, and while he brushes away, we can go to our old haunts and look at the valleys and throw stones at the monkeys like we used to do. Three nights? Can you get away?"

He must have known that I had to tell some sort of lie at home to be absent for that period during the impending school holidays, but he never enquired as to what subterfuge I had used.

I had to be more conniving this time. I took some St Anselm's notepaper from Father Simeon's rooms and approached Vasco with it.

"You have to do me a favour so I can go with you and Father on our holiday," I said.

"Like what, men?" he asked.

"Write a note from, let us say, Dr De Cruz, saying he requires me to attend a geological school trip for four days and requiring my mummy or daddy's signature."

"That is a sin," Vasco said.

"A lot of things are sins, Vasco. What are you doing, casting the first stone?"

"We are brothers in sin, boss, of course I will write it in good calligraphic hand," he said and grinned.

"And no word to Father, okay?"

He shook his head and got down to writing as I dictated.

Mummy didn't read English so my sister read it to her, and she looked doubtful and questioned me about the geological trip and with whom and how many boys and so on and then signed it in English, her signature being the one graphic she had, for official reasons, learned to execute. The acceptance note was supposedly returned to Dr De Cruz. I tore it up and threw it in the gutter that flowed under the tiny brick bridge on the way to school.

Father Simeon drove the three of us in the old school van, and we pitched two tents by a river.

"You boys are in the big one and I'll have the other to my old self," he said. "Do you mind?"

"*Je m'en fou*!" said Vasco.

"That's not very nice," Father said. So Vasco was picking up French phrases.

I was happy with the arrangement. I didn't want to share a tent with Vasco, but at least they didn't assume that they were sharing a tent and leaving me out of it.

My contentment with the arrangement was short-lived. We had spent the first day on the tracks looking at the valleys and woods, and when we got back to our unguarded camp it was night. We cooked over a fire, which Father Simeon lit expertly from the twigs we had gathered, and after the campfire dinner decided it was bedtime. He turned to Vasco.

"You must come and give me some help with the batteries, *mon petit*, and we must distribute the water for the night," he said.

Vasco changed into his pyjamas, hiding his body from my eyes with a wrapped towel, and then without a word he left me to slip into my bedding and went off to the other tent. I strained my ears for sounds. I heard low murmurings. They were whispering. In half an hour Vasco came back. I pretended to be asleep, and he slipped into his bedding and in seconds was asleep. A deep satisfied sleep? Unlike mine?

In the early morning, we washed by the river and struck camp. Father Simeon said we were moving on and without telling us where, he drove us out past Khandala on to the dirt tracks that led to the forest and the cliffs and then to the Duke's Nose. When the van went as far as it could go, he got out and surveyed the route.

"You know the path through, don't you, *mes enfants*?"

"I've never been here before," Vasco said.

"We can leave the van here, and a few hundred yards in there's the waterfall, let's see if we can get comfortable there."

"Shall I unload the tents?" I asked.

"No, you have to take the maestro to the high point."

"What high point?" the "maestro" asked.

"Pervez will take you," Father said.

Now his intent became clear as paints and board and the stretched canvas and portable easel were unloaded from the van. I was to take Vasco to the Duke's Nose, and he was to spend the rest of the day and perhaps the next day painting his view of the valleys and woods and hillsides from the Duke's Nose.

"Rich as Claude Monet," Father Simeon said. He kissed Vasco on the forehead, and we set off. He would set up the tents, he said, and that's where we were to come when we descended.

"Look into the sunset and capture what you can of the light over the distant Arabian Sea as it goes down into the water, but don't linger. Take the torches and don't get caught in the dark. It'll be a half hour between the rock and our camp." He waved as we trekked away wordlessly.

We got to the rock and edged our way along the cantilevered bit over the deep valley. I helped Vasco set up the easel and stretched canvas. He spent a half hour just looking, saying nothing. We both looked across the clear landscape of forest and the clouds towards where the coast should be, forty miles away. They would perhaps clear by the afternoon as the sea heat forced them to rise, and we would get a glimpse of the waters.

"That drop could kill you, bossy," Vasco said, looking down the precipice.

"It could," I said. "It does. A lot of lovers who are forbidden by their parents or something come here and jump off. Their bodies are never found. Or if they are found, they've been picked clean by jackals and vultures, and no one can make out which was the boy and which was the girl."

Vasco listened to this grim tale, and then he took out his paints from the canvas bag he had carried on his back.

"Too much to paint here, boss, must choose the focus properly. We are coming back tomorrow, no?"

He took out a thick pencil and began making marks on the canvas.

As he did, one of the legs of the easel began to slip on the rock, and he grabbed the canvas. I leapt forward and stopped the easel from falling.

"Hold it there, I'll get a rock to stop it sliding," I said.

I had to get off the smooth and narrow top of the Nose to find loose rocks and returned with two big ones with vaguely concave bottoms so they would hold the wooden spar of the easel firmly. It was a good fit, and Vasco tried its strength and firmness and nodded.

"You got it, yaar!"

As God is my witness, I had not thought of it before that moment. I was now lying on my belly on the big rock having adjusted the small rocks at the foot of the easel. Vasco's tennis shoes were a foot away from my face.

"You," I said, lying there flat and stable. "You know that since you came to the school things have changed for me?"

"No, no, how could I," he said, stepping back so he could see my upturned face. His body was framed against the sky behind him and then the sheer drop of two thousand feet through brush and rock-face.

"How could I notice the change if I wasn't there before?"

"Trying to be smart with me?" I asked. "You know fucking well what I mean."

"I didn't know you were fucking well," he said and laughed, thinking I'd join in.

He obviously hadn't picked up on the hoarse and hesitant breathlessness of my voice. My heart was beating faster, and I was looking at his worn tennis shoes, which he wore without socks.

"Don't fuck about with your jokes. I mean with Father Simeon," I said. The last phrase came out choked.

"Pervez, believe me, I know what you mean but stop; you are wrong."

"I am not wrong. You came like a thief and stole him from me."

"No, boss, I swear I am looking after him, just looking after him."

"Don't lie! He is either going to be your special friend or mine."

"Eh, don't be silly, yaar!" he said.

He was now aware that he stood between my prone self and the precipice, and before he could escape from that predicament, I grabbed the ankle of his right foot and lifted it off the ground so he would lose his balance. He hopped and staggered and fell backwards.

"What's to stop me throwing you and the fucking painting off the rock? Accident. You slipped."

"No, please, Pervez. Listen, spare me … please … I am begging … He is not yours or mine. He now belongs to Christ."

"Don't try and talk yourself…" I said.

"He is going to die. He's got cancer in the brain. He'll die any day. Please don't do this. Spare me, and I'll never tell anyone."

One push and he would go head-first to his death. He had stopped struggling and placed his faith in my conscience.

"Cancer?"

"Yes, a brain tumour. He knows he is finished. He is going to a hospice and wanted this painting for his last hours."

I released my grip and slid backwards. Vasco scrambled to his feet and ran to the safety of the cliff edge, leaving the easel.

"You are not lying?" I asked.

He wasn't. I knew he wasn't because my insides had leapt to my mouth and there was an emptiness behind my chest and stomach.

He shook his head sadly.

"You won't tell anybody about any of this?" I asked.

"Of course not. I know you love him, but so do I, and he loves us both, and now he can't have either. He sometimes thinks it's a punishment from God who still thinks ... who still thinks what we do, because we are boys, is a sin."

"God doesn't think that," I said. "And Father definitely knows that people have wilfully misunderstood St Paul and the other prophets. If two people love each other, God will bless whatever they do with each other; after all, it's only bodies, dust into dust."

"You've been discussing the same thing that we've been discussing," Vasco said. "I know it all by heart."

"You said he was going..."

"Yes, as soon as we get back. The pain is too much, and he can't kill himself. I went to his tent yesterday to give him an injection, men. He has these injections now more and more. For pain. We didn't tell you because he doesn't want to make you sad."

"Where will he go?"

"The Order has places for Jesuits to go and die in peace. Nasik, he said."

I knew he was telling the truth, and I felt like a fool. I wanted to ask his forgiveness but instead I said, "Start the painting. Do it from a different point. I'll pull the easel in, so there won't even be any accidents."

Vasco finished the painting of the view from the Duke's Nose in the next two days. We saw the sunsets and the smooth singeing of the waters as the orange ball fell into the sea.

Father Simeon didn't know that we had talked. He had sworn Vasco to secrecy.

When we got back to Poona on the fourth night, he kissed me in the dark outside the van and said he was now going on a long journey.

My daddy had met Mr De Cruz in the baker's shop on East Street and said he thought he was away on a geology trip with some boys. Mr De Cruz was taken aback and assured Daddy that he was right there in the bakery buying Shrewsbury biscuits for his wife and children because they were going for their school holidays to relatives in Bombay. He knew nothing about a geology trip.

Daddy was waiting for me with a belt.

"Where have you been?"

"The geology trip. A lot of hard work and great science, gathering samples, digging..."

"How you lie to your mummy and daddy, you bastard!" He lashed out at me with his belt and struck me first across my face and then across my arm.

Mummy leapt in.

"Tehmtan, stop, stop, you'll kill him. Stop! Please stop."

Daddy didn't stop. He pushed her aside with his left arm and continued to bring the strap swishing down on me.

"You dog, you eat my food and then you lie to me and get up to monkey business with your filthy priests and gutter boys?"

I stood absolutely still, covering my burning face with my arms in a sort of boxer's crouch. I wasn't going to run from his whip. I had asked for it. Mummy came back at him and grabbed the belt from his hand. Then the strangest thing happened. My father burst into tears. She held him as he sobbed.

"What will I tell people? How can I tell the world what my only son is? That he lends himself to men, to grown, old, filthy men? That I sent him to that school to become this?"

She hushed him and led him away.

I left the house and went back to the school. It was dark, but there was sound of a chant coming from the first floor and Father Simeon's rooms were brightly lit. On the dark staircase I found Vasco.

"He's gone. Gone to Christ. The Padris are in there. God knows what they are doing with his body."

That was the last time I saw Vasco.

Mummy, if you are reading this to this point you can understand that without Father Simeon, with no friends, without Daddy and you, I have no life. I am nobody. *Tant pis*. This is why I am going to do what you will know I have done. Did I mean Madame Bovary or that other Russian book Father Simeon told us about—*Anna Karenina*? I can't think now. Anyway, what does it matter?

Thank you for my happy life.

Pervez

*

The above account, scribbled on notepaper, was left in the empty waiting room of the abandoned platform on the edge of the ghats that used to be Khandala station. The police said he had broken into it and perhaps spent a night or two there. The papers were found and handed to his mother.

They identified the body, which was badly mutilated and chopped in two after the wheels of the Deccan Queen had gone over it.

*

(Miriam: A letter from the mum of the friend whose suicide letter I imaginatively wrote about—good for the Second Edition? – fd)

I translate as best as I can and literally from the Gujarati:

"My dear Farokh (sic),

How I can call you these things is also very difficult and making me choke on my words. How could you do this terrible thing to your great friend and childhood playmate, my only dear dead departed Pervez. We always thought of you as his best friend even though you were then going to different schools because of your parents being so stuck-up and having some money. God blesses the poor more.

Pervez's passing away has left us only with our two daughters and the great stone of grief on our heads and shoulders and chests and there is nothing left in life even though now there are grandchildren. I have never put my dear son out of my thoughts or heart and all we have is memories. Such lovely memories.

I trusted you when I gave the last will and testament papers that poor Pervez left before the train accident and you have now printed them and distorted them and brought the memory of our lovely boy into disrepute. When you read these things you must think to yourself that perhaps everything the person is writing cannot be just like that. Some is imagination, some comes from what other people are saying and everything like that. You are making out in your book, whose passages about Pervez my daughter and my granddaughter read out to me in English and then Gujarati, that he was doing things with the Father and the boy Vasco. What kind of reputation do you think he will have now? How can his poor father who is suffering acutely from marble in the eye ever face another day or our relatives?

Didn't you think before you wrote these things and used the papers, that I willingly from my heart gave you to see, thinking that you will preserve the great memory of our dear son for us and others, to hurt people and destroy goodness in this way? By writing wretched things.

How I really feel is that curses come to my tongue to wish you in suffering and hell but I am a woman of prayer and won't say them, though God knows I have thought them a hundred times since finding out what you have written and betrayed our darling Pervez and his memory.

Your former neighbour,
Pirojbai (Pee aunty)

*

Dear Pee Aunty,

I am so glad I found you or that indeed you found me.

I am only writing back to say that you are completely wrong about the episode I included in my book quoting my friend, yes, my friend, Pervez's last written statement.

I was very careful to leave out the very intimate descriptions he gave and the guilt he felt. Ask your daughter or a neutral party to read the letter he left (which by the way was *not* addressed to you but was a general address to whom, as it were, it may concern. I feel, as you must, that it was basically addressed to you, but in any formal or legal sense, it was public property and there must have been a part of Pervez, if I knew him at all, who wanted the world to know what he confessed to!)

As I said I left out the bits in which he expresses his deep jealousy and writes very explicit passages about the fears and fantasies of what he thinks Vasco has seduced Father Simeon into doing. If I had wanted notoriety as you seem to accuse me of doing, I would have left these in.

The other thing I cut out was the passage about the gold ring inscribed with "Ad Majorem Dei Gloriam" which he says Father Simeon gave him on their "engagement". I surmised that either this large and probably 24-carat ring was stolen from Pervez's finger by whoever found the body or that it was still on his body when you were asked to identify and retrieve it and so might be something you have acquired. The ring probably belongs to the school or the Jesuitical church and I wasn't sure how Pervez acquired it and so thought it best to leave the passage about the ring out. My advice is don't attempt to sell it to a market trader as it may have been reported as not quite regular.

If I have offended you, I sincerely beg your pardon but to tell the truth, I and the generations that follow won't react with any shock or horror to Pervez's story even while they feel the waste, the pathos and the tragedy of it.

Yours ever,
Farrukh

Birds And Bees

My mother's cousin Armity came from the small town where she lived to see her family in Poona. My mother and aunts picked her up from the railway station and brought her in a caravan of three horse-drawn tongas home.

We hadn't been warned about her appearance or her ways of expression and voice. She was very pretty with perfectly cut short hair, but she had a harelip and cleft palate. She spoke with a nasal sound, which we as children had to get used to in order to grasp what she was saying. Even the first kiss, the bending down and grabbing me with a greeting that must have been "How big you've grown since I last saw you," or "You obviously don't remember me," sounded like stray unmelodic notes of a mouth organ. I didn't know what she was saying but knew that it would be impolite to admit that I couldn't follow it.

She had come to Poona because my family had, through distant relatives, found a young man who knew of her disability but had indicated through the negotiations that he was willing to consider her as a prospective bride.

My sister and I were asked to vacate our bedroom, which was no more than a curtained-off section of a larger room, in order to accommodate this new "aunt". She was charming and bright-eyed, and we didn't resent the temporary move to mattresses in the front room in the least.

The family of the prospective husband was to come to tea, and as we watched the preparations, my sister and I saw Armity sitting nervously in front of the dressing-table mirror in my aunt's room, contriving to disguise her harelip with lipstick and powder around the scar. I felt for her. She had startling eyes and a dainty nose, but the gash and then her uncertain nasal tones when she spoke left me with a sinking feeling. She was selling herself, and that my mother's cousin had to stoop to this made me ashamed.

The family in the person of two stern older women and the prospective husband and a teenaged brother turned up and were shown into the front room from which our mattresses had been removed. They were served tea by the cook who was made to wear a jacket for the occasion. Armity, as is the custom, was asked to bring in the tray of treats, which she was to claim she had cooked though most of the cooking had been done by my mother and her sisters.

The prospective husband sat straight-backed in one of the wooden-framed chairs with the woven cane seats and backs that adorned our front room. The portraits of my ancestors, the men moustached and wearing cylindrical felt Parsi hats, the women in brocade saris striking various poses of piety and seriousness, looked down upon us from the heights at which they were hung. My father had declined to attend the gathering, and my mother, after introducing us to this party of surveillance, asked us to leave the room, to go and study or play or whatever.

The Prospective's party left after tea. My father returned and there ensued what sounded to us like a terrible row. My sister peeked round the door of my grandfather's bedroom where the family was gathered, and which we were forbidden to enter, and said that Armity was in tears and my aunt had her arm around her.

"You think any decent person could ask that?" we heard my father shout. "How dare you even talk to such people."

My mother's reply was inaudible, but its tone was unmistakably pleading.

"If there is any more talk of examinations, I will leave the house, I tell you!" my father shouted.

Again some female voices seemed to attempt to ameliorate his anger or annoyance. They were too soft for me to hear what was actually said.

Whatever it was it couldn't have helped because my father came out of the room, banging the door behind him.

He found us in poses of eavesdropping, and we thought he would vent his anger on us, but he hadn't finished what he had to say back in the family gathering, and so he said it now to us.

"What will people think? That this family has no shame? That we are desperate to find some idiot whose mind is still in the primitive ages? Ask your mother, ask your aunts how anyone is daring enough to believe we have come to this!"

He walked out, we presumed, to the front veranda and then out of the house.

I did ask my mother what the matter was and prefaced it by saying that Dad had asked me to enquire.

Surprisingly, my mother with a very solemn face asked my sister and me to go to her bedroom. She said she'd tell us.

What she said didn't startle or surprise me in the least, but my sister was appalled and horrified. My mother had determined to tell us, for the first time, about sex and where babies came from and one of the purposes of marriage.

I had exchanged erroneous information about these matters endlessly in school and with my male friends and cousins. I knew that my sister and girl cousins knew nothing of these matters, and at that age I felt I would do battle to keep all knowledge of such filth from them.

And now here was my mother explaining the same matters as delicately as she could without the aid of illustrations or a book with simple diagrams (perhaps none existed in that day and age). She didn't allude to the pleasure of sex but talked about love and it leading to particular intimacy and how seeds and eggs had to come together to make babies, which then grew in the mother's womb and not as we had always loosely believed in the "stomach".

"Then why was Aunty Armity crying and why was Daddy shouting?" my sister asked.

"I think he was right to shout," our mother said.

"But why was Aunty Armity sad?" I asked.

"She wasn't sad, she was hurt and frightened." My mother was distinctly wondering whether she should complete what she had begun. After all, the lesson in procreation was intended to explain in some measure the incidents of that evening.

"I'll tell you," she said. "You see, those people who came to see Armity had been told that she was born with the sort of lip and palate and speech defects that we all know about. The gentleman who came said he didn't mind any of that, but that was before he came here and saw her. We had told him that the doctors who had seen her when she was born and a few years after said nothing could be done about any of it, and she would have to live with it. You've seen what a pretty lady your aunty is and well educated and gentle and sweet."

We listened and Mum searched our faces, probably wondering how far she would be violating our innocence.

"Well, this man and perhaps his mother and his aunt were not prepared for what they were going to see. When they saw Armity, some silly idea came into their heads. They thought that if she had something wrong with her lips and mouth, then maybe she would have something wrong with other parts of her body also. So they discussed it in whispers together for just one minute, and then they asked me if they could examine Aunty Armity before they made up their minds to let the son get engaged to her."

"What did they want to examine?" my sister asked, frowning.

"Her whole body," Mum said, but my sister continued to frown.

"The part that makes babies, you fool," I said.

"You mean…?" And my sister pointed very hastily to her own crotch. "To look?"

"Yes. It was a very foolish thing to ask, and all I and your other aunties could say was that this was not something we could think of or discuss. And then your aunty Shera said perhaps we should give them a doctor's report."

"So are you giving them a doctor's report?"

"I don't think so. That was quite wrong even though this fellow's aunts looked at each other and thought that would be sufficient. Armity was very confused and started crying as soon as we told her. We had to tell her. She was going to say that she wouldn't mind having a doctor's report, but before she could even say that your dad came home, and we told him the whole story, and then you heard what happened. He was furious and banged about and said that that family ought to be lined up against the wall and shot and … you know what happens when your dad gets really angry."

"So what will happen now?" my sister asked.

"Then where will you go?" she was asked.

"I'll have to wander about and find another road that they are building and ask the foreman if they need my labour," she said.

She took her bundle and went looking for the next road to build but returned that night to our veranda, which she must have thought of as the only hospitable spot in the city.

"Why don't you stay here, forget labouring and look after our children as their ayah," my grandmother offered.

Chandri was delighted.

The family was told her story. She was from a village about fifty miles away, an isolated village, accessible not even by a bullock cart and only by foot. She was born there and at the age of nine or so was married to a man thirty years older. She said she and her people didn't keep records of birthdates so she couldn't even say precisely how old she was. She told my grandmother that she got pregnant as soon as she was fertile in her early teens, but lost the child through a miscarriage. She said she bled copiously and nobody cared. There was no doctor or medical facility in the village, and her husband's family were not good to her. They said they'd leave her to die because she was of no use to them if she couldn't bear children. But she didn't die and when she recovered, went back to virtual slavery in her husband's house.

The year before she came to the town to work on the road a plague of smallpox came to their village. Her husband caught the disease and died as did his younger brother. Their mother turned on Chandri, saying she had brought the disease to the house, that she was a witch, and the only thing she could do to purify her soul was to commit sati on the funeral pyre of her husband.

Chandri ran away and came to the city and found the labouring job. She knew nobody outside her village, and she couldn't return there for fear she'd be killed, stoned to death or burnt alive as a *churail*, an evil spirit in the shape of a woman with its feet turned backwards, because the rest of the villagers had been convinced by her mother-in-law that she had brought the misfortune of the disease on them.

With defiance in her eyes she now told my grandmother that she was of the Mahar caste, an untouchable by birth, and that she was quite prepared to leave if that's what the lady of the house desired and decreed. She was waiting, my grandmother said for a reaction, uncertain as to whether this confession would cause her to be turned away. My grandfather was called in to adjudicate because the information was not something my grandmother understood. She had no idea what the Mahar caste was.

Ardeshir Antia, however, was employed by the Land Revenue Records service and knew precisely what it meant.

"We are Parsis, not Hindus," he told Chandri. "We don't have any castes, don't believe in any of that nonsense and don't care what caste you are. If my wife thinks you are suitable, that's all. You are welcome here."

Chandri settled into being one of the family. She had a room, which was no more than an enclosed space on the back veranda of the house, similar to the space I occupied a generation later. She looked after the children of the joint family and then, when my grandfather's brother found employment in Bombay and eventually took his family to settle in the big city, she became exclusive ayah to my mother, her three sisters and, when he was born, their youngest brother.

My mother was in her late twenties when she got married. Chandri was still with the household in Poona. There were no children to look after any more as my uncle was now of college-going age. She would help my grandma around the house and had by now assumed charge of many aspects of the household's affairs. She would bargain with the travelling peddlers of eggs and vegetables, and she would spy on the cook whom she said she suspected of selling off part of the consignment of coal that was bought in sacks for cooking and heating our bathwater in the speckled metal-jacket boiler that stood on a three-footed trestle in the backyard. She also loved, groomed and bathed the several dogs that the household had been lumbered with.

When my sister was born, my parents were in an army house in Kirkee, the adjoining town to Poona Cantonment, and without being asked or ordered, Chandri assumed that she was now naturally attached to my mother and father's family and was to assume, as a grandmother would, the duty of looking after my sister Zareen. There was no resisting her. She told my mother that she wouldn't allow any young whipper-snapper of a Goan ayah to usurp her rightful place, and she left my grandmother's and moved in to the Kirkee house, surveying the detached rooms of the servants' quarters behind the house to see which accommodation suited her best.

After I was born, Chandri travelled with my mother and father to Quetta. She was illiterate. But besides the Marathi and Gujarati songs she sang to us she had, through my sister's baby years, picked up the sounds of the nursery rhymes and lullabies my mother would sing. She didn't have a very accurate ear and would sing,

> "*Goni Bhai Raabi shin*
> *Tho Ratna baby Bunchhee*" to render
>
> "Gone to buy a rabbit skin
> To wrap my baby bunting in."

We knew what she was singing as she patted us to sleep in our woolly pyjamas on cold nights when the hills beyond our house would come alive with the howls of wolves and keep us awake with fear.

Our teddy bears were "teddy-beck" and a shower was a "saavak". She was a granny to us, and we should have respectfully called her Chandrabai, but the name Chandri had stuck and when I, in some self-consciousness about respect, ventured to try the proper name she muttered her objection.

"What's this 'Chandrabai'? Have I become your grandmother or what?"

So Chandri it was till she died.

She went all around India from Madras and Cochin in the south to Kashmir in the north with my parents, and when my sister and I had grown out of her hands, she took charge of our new sister who was ten years younger than me.

Sometimes we said to ourselves that fate had taken Chandri on a strange ride. The girl from the Karla hills where her village was would never have contemplated living in six cities of India, seeing palaces and the Taj Mahal, military tattoos and the mountains and passes of Kashmir—where she refused to eat strawberries because they were a strange fruit.

When my parents packed their belongings and moved from one army station to another, Chandri would help pack the crates of kitchenware and crockery, and on the last day when we caught the military train from one or other station platform, she would run along it in her cotton sari shouting, "surrvan dubba, surrvan dubba!" wanting someone to direct her to the servant carriage reserved, as in the days of the Raj, for the domestic employees of the regiment's officers. When the train took an extended stop on the long, inevitably overnight and sometimes two-or-three-night journeys, she would come and eat with us and bring her bedding into our compartment and spread it on the floor.

The six nights on the train that Chandri always recalled were those she spent with my mother, my sister and I, aged five and three; when we had to journey in an army-guarded train with other Indian army officers' families across the newly drawn border of Pakistan and India.

My father had been posted to Quetta before Partition, and when the resentment of those who had been displaced by the partition of the subcontinent on both sides turned into slaughter, he had been called away to Naushera in what became Pakistan, still under British Raj command, to enforce martial law and keep such peace as could be kept. My mother and Chandri were left to board the army train that would wend its way to India taking six tortuous days for a journey that could have taken a day and a half.

The train compartment had heavy double shutters, the first of glass and the second of metal shaped with a cascade of vents to let the air through. These were pulled down as the train progressed, sealing the passengers off from the sight but not the sounds of the carnage outside. Trails of refugees were crossing the border, Muslims whose lands had been grabbed and who had been terrorized away from it were travelling westward to what was to be Pakistan, and Hindus and Sikhs were moving eastward away from the same barbarism to homeless and penniless safety.

I have no recollection of that journey though I can remember scenes and incidents from my short life before it. The howling of wolves at night, the tree outside the kitchen window that grew the green pointed bean I had put in my mouth against all caution and howled to high heaven when it stung my mouth, the crushed ice-and-syrup lollies my visiting grandfather made and stuck on sticks as a treat for us; the terror that struck me on seeing the officers who had dressed as clowns with painted faces to amuse the children at the army fete; the porcupine that curled into a spiky ball by the stream that ran through the wilderness behind our house … but no memory of that journey through the corridor of slaughter.

Chandri told us in later life what our mother wouldn't. She said she saw the trails of refugees, thousands upon thousands of people crossing both ways, using the railway line as a guide to direction, knowing it would take them to chartered towns and cities. She said she saw them rush at each other with swords and cudgels and that she saw the murder of men, women and children on a scale we couldn't imagine. She had seen gangs of warriors, Sikhs who rode horses and carried drawn and bloody swords, men who had taken an oath to protect their own from the enemy and had exceeded their oath by killing innocents progressing with their pathetic bundles and belongings in the other direction. She said one train that they crossed was full of dead bodies.

My mother told us that the train we were on progressed from the new border to Delhi and there she and the other army wives on the train at last felt safe. Nothing. I remember nothing of the danger or the relief.

Chandri accompanied my mother, father and younger sister to Delhi when Dad was transferred to the capital. They set up house in one of the then new developments called Defence Colony. I was in college in Bombay, and when I could stand the study of chemical engineering no longer, I said goodbye to my bewildered granduncle with whom I lived, declined his offer of money and took my chances by riding ticketless to Delhi on the train.

I knew the address in Delhi and made my way home. My mother was surprised to see me and only then told me that my father was in the military hospital having a kidney operation and wouldn't be back for a couple of weeks at least as some complications had set in. They hadn't written to me or to the rest of the family as they didn't want to worry anyone. I had to visit him that afternoon and tell him that I had run away from college and didn't intend to go back and complete my engineering degree course. He wasn't pleased. It wasn't the sort of concern or care I should have burdened him with when he was ill, but there was no avoiding it.

"So what do you think you'll do?" he asked, absorbing the information, and his brow telling me it was a worry he could have done without.

"I don't know," I said. "But I can't see myself manufacturing chemicals for the rest of my life."

"So what are you going to do that's better? Who's put these stupid ideas in your head?"

"I think it was D.H. Lawrence," I said.

"You're talking nonsense again," he said. "This is the kind of insolence that will get you into trouble."

We agreed that I would think about my future, and we would discuss it when he came out of hospital. He was in too much pain to give it proper thought or to assert the authority he unquestionably had in the family.

I spent my days reading the books I bought from pavement booksellers—Penguin editions of Hemingway, Faulkner, Lawrence, second-hand editions of Bergson and George Santayana, the cheap editions of communist literature published by the Soviet press and anything else I could get my hands on. I was beginning to make sense of what I was reading though I am sure today that I couldn't have grasped the whole meaning of the Nietzsche tracts or of Bergson or the translation of Immanuel Kant that I attempted and pretended to absorb.

Chandri looked after my younger sister and helped Mum with the cooking and cleaning. She slept in the detached room in the small paved yard, and she hated Delhi. She wouldn't venture further than the tiny park to which she took my sister in the evenings before sunset to play with other children of the colony. She said she didn't understand the language as she spoke only Marathi, and Hindi was the lingua franca of Delhi. The only Hindi phrase she had picked up was "I don't understand or speak Hindi" and she had turned a word or two of that into Marathi so the statement that she didn't understand wouldn't have been understood.

Chandri would be the first to wake up each morning, and she'd make tea and wake my mother up and then my sister to bathe and dress for school. They'd leave me asleep knowing I would have been reading into the small hours. One morning my mother woke me saying, "Something's happened to Chandri. Come down. I can't wake her up."

I ran down in my pyjamas into the yard and into her room. The room stank of the tobacco she used to chew and spit into a brass vessel. She slept on a mattress in the corner, and this day she lay on it, still on her side. We called out to her.

I put my hand to her nose and felt no inhalation of breath. Her lungs were still. I lifted her limp arm and felt her pulse. Nothing. Her eyes were shut. I shouted into her ear.

"Chandrabai! No!"

I turned to my mother who had tears down her cheeks.

"She's dead," I said.

"Shall we call a doctor?" my mother asked.

"Do we know a doctor? Nothing will be open this time of the morning."

"There's Dr Sawhney whom we meet in the park. He's always very nice. He lives in the next block somewhere."

"I'll go," I said.

I put on a shirt and was going to run out barefoot in my pyjamas but stopped myself. What was the hurry? I was certain she was dead. Calling a doctor was a gesture to put an official seal on it.

I looked for the house. It was not yet seven in the morning, and only the milkmen and some vendors of vegetables were stirring. A cycle-rickshaw lazed its way past me. I got to the next block where the houses were larger, some with slumbering sentries in wooden boxes outside their gates.

I searched the nameplates and found the one I was looking for. It said "Dr V.D. Sawhney, Dr Mrs J.V. Sawhney, Dr T.V. Sawhney, Dr Miss S.V. Sawhney". A medical family, no less.

I opened the gate and rang the bell. A servant answered. I asked for Dr V.D. Sawhney. He came out in a kurta and pyjama and I told him that we thought our servant, the lady whom he knew from the park when he took his evening walk, was either very sick or dead.

He said he'd come immediately and went in to change into street clothes and get his shoes.

It took him a few seconds to pronounce her dead. Liquids were now drooling out of her mouth.

"She will be unclean, the body relaxes and all the valves give way. It's not pleasant," he said.

"Don't worry, doctor. Thank you. I'd do anything for her," my mother said.

"What do we do with her?" I asked.

He immediately knew what I meant.

"She was a Hindu?"

"She ... was," my mother said.

"Call the Delhi Municipality. They have a service attached to hospitals to convey dead bodies to the graveyards or burning ghats by the river. They will take care of it," he said. "I'll do it for you," he added. "Where's the phone?"

Late that morning the grey van arrived. A gaunt man in a grey shirt accompanied by a short man with a hunchback who could have been a robust teenager or a much older, stunted individual, came in bearing a stretcher. My mother had taken buckets of hot water into the yard and cleaned Chandri up and wrapped her in a couple of washed cotton saris. The men hoisted the body onto the stretcher.

"You go," my mother said. "I'd better take Baby to school and then I can join you by rickshaw."

We asked where she would be taken and the driver gave us the address.

I sat with the two of them in the front of the van with the body in the back. The driver wanted to chat.

"Who was she? Was she a relative?"

"She was like my grandmother," I said.

"But you are so fair, she is dark, no?"

"Adopted grandmother," I said.

"I understand. I thought she was a servant at first, sir."

"She was part of the household and yes she did work for the family."

"That's very good and where is your father?"

"He's an army man. He's in the hospital for a few days," I replied though I didn't see why I should.

I looked at the short man with the protruding bone in his back. He had a long sad face and was wearing a large olive-green army surplus shirt with its epaulets cut off. He smiled, a small, sad smile. It could have been part of his funereal manner or an expression of resignation to his fate.

The driver saw me looking at him and now lapsed from polite Hindi into English.

"Him is brother. Not orderly. Them is give one driver one orderly, like this." He pinched the front of his grey jacket to indicate that it was a supplied uniform. "My orderly bastard man just going holiday today. Saying wife serious. All lies things. For service for you I brings my brother."

"That's good of you," I said.

"Well, well," he said. "Well, well, well, well—well!"

He had obviously picked up the expression from someone but hadn't mastered its deployment. He said it to fill the silence. He was formulating his next English sentence.

"He is very good servant. Called Abdul."

Abdul nodded sadly in assent. Yes, that was what he was called.

"You must be needing servant now when old lady is pass away," the driver said. "He will be taking small salary and does everythings."

I didn't know what to say. We had driven off the main road and were being signposted down lanes to the banks of the river where the burning ghats for the cremation of the dead were. We drove through large gateposts that didn't seem to have gates attached to them.

"What you say, sir, you have Abdul? My brother," the driver said, reluctant to let this opportunity for employment for his brother pass.

"No, no. I can't think of that today," I said.

"You living Defence. Father in hospital. Must to be able paying good salary. We come tomorrow," he persisted.

I opened the van door and got out saying, "No, please don't come tomorrow, we don't need any servants."

"Day after tomorrow? Ask mummy," he said, opening the back doors of the van to take out the body of Chandri, her face and body covered now with the regulation dirty muslin cloth they had in the van.

"Any day we can come," he said.

"No, no day. Just do what you have to do now," I said.

A Brahmin priest had seen the van and the bier carried by the two men and he approached us.

"Forty rupees for wood and twenty for service," he said to me without any preliminaries.

"Yes, if that's what needs to be done," I said.

The driver and his brother Abdul carried Chandri's body to a waiting pyre of wood. There were other pyres burning, crackling in the sun. The filthy river flowed sluggishly twenty feet away from them. They picked up the body, respectfully I thought, and placed it on the pyre. The Brahmin supervised.

The driver stood staring at me when they were done, holding the muslin sheet he had taken off, exposing Chandri's face.

"That's it, go now," the priest said to them in Hindi. His tone implied that he was taking over from here on.

He turned to me. "Rascal is wanting tip. Him is get good government money. Give nothing," he said.

I gave the two of them ten rupees each for which they seemed grateful.

"So no servant wanting?" He was making a last try.

I shook my head. He shrugged, and the pair of them turned and went back to the van.

"Rascals," the priest said. "You want first-class funeral."

"Is there a second-class one?" I asked.

"Of course there is," he said. "But your amma need first class."

He explained to me that the body would take a whole day and night to burn, and the ashes could be taken away the next day or even the day after.

Two men came and hovered around.

"Do you want to buy bed to send to heaven with your loved mother-lady?" one of the men asked. "With mattress two hundred rupees."

"Saris? What will she wear in heaven?" the other said.

I wanted to tell them to fuck off.

"She'll only be wearing wings, now get away from me, you vultures!"

They looked at each other. A tough customer. They walked off.

My mother arrived driven by Gita, a young neighbour who had seen the van and Chandri's body being loaded into it and had come round to help. They came down the stone steps and I explained to them what was going on.

The ceremony began, and the priest asked me if I was her son. I said I was an adopted son, and he seemed happy with that. Another priest joined him. They poured oil and threw what I thought were sandalwood flakes on the pyre. The second priest lit a torch of what seemed like hay and handed it to me. I was to walk around the pyre and then light it. My mum was crying and through her sobs was saying our Zoroastrian prayers.

I lit the pyre. The fellows who had offered me the bed and the clothes to send to heaven stood by and were about to petition my mother with the same offers, perhaps at a concessional price. I lit the pyre and with the torch still alight in my hand went up to them.

"I told you to fuck off," I said menacingly.

One of them grinned. He wasn't going to be intimidated by a beardless teenage boy. They walked slowly away towards another funeral pyre that was being prepared a hundred yards away down-river.

"Money in advance," the priest said, though strictly speaking the procedure was well under way.

My mother paid him what he asked for.

"Body will sometimes be looking like sitting up and again falling so don't be alarm," he said. "Bring pots tomorrow. Brass pots!"

There were benches provided, but we went a little way down the river and sat on some rocks watching the pyre burn and the smoke ascending.

"Is there anything more to do?" Mum asked.

"Nothing. But I want to wait here. I'll come back tonight. You should go, you are keeping Gita from her work and you have to pick up Baby from school."

My mother and Gita left.

I walked along the bank of the Yamuna. Some people had brought a body in a funeral procession and were setting it afloat on a sort of wooden raft on the waters, wading out towards the middle of the river to make sure it caught the current.

By sunset the cremation ghat was deserted. The priests had been a few times and poured oil on the burning pyres to keep them going.

I thought of walking up the lane and finding conveyance home. A lone man with a long beard in a white gown and kind but piercing eyes sat on a rock as I looked for a way to scramble up the banks. He called out to me.

"Your relative?" he asked in English.

"Yes," I said.

"Gone in a day. Ashes," he said. "Vanity. It's all vanity. Your food and drink and sex and even your education and your religion, it's all vanity."

I didn't know why he was saying it or what he wanted from me.

"These mutterings. No one is listening, you know." He perhaps wanted to engage me in a debate.

"Did you come to cremate a relative?" I asked.

"No," he said. "I come here every day. Then I get weak and go back to where I can eat and drink. I want to get the strength to come and sit here and go nowhere and starve myself to death." He was serious.

"Yeah, okay," was all I could say. I hastened away, scrambling up the muddy bank. I heard him laugh out loud behind me.

My mother and I brought my sister the next evening. Neither I nor my mum could remember which of the pyres was Chandri's. They had been piled high with wood and flames the day before and were now beds of ashes. The priest directed us to the right one. The ashes were still warm when I scooped them into a brass urn, which we used in the house as a vase.

"She always said to me that she wanted her ashes deposited in the river that ran by her village. It was her only wish, really, and she used to joke about it. She said she'd only return to her village in a casket," my mum said.

We kept the ashes in the vase for the next few months. Dad came out of the hospital and was convalescing at home. It was decided after long discussions that I would go back to Poona, rejoin my old college having surrendered a year to "foolishness" as Dad put it, and complete a bachelor of science degree with physics as my principal subject. The urn was carefully secured with a cloth bung tied to the top, and I took it in my luggage to Poona. I would take Chandri's ashes to the river where she wanted them deposited.

My uncle recalled the name she used for her village. It was called Karvanjilla, but we couldn't find it on even the one-inch survey maps in the Bombay public library. No one seemed to know how to get to it, but the family remembered that Chandri had always said it was near or downhill from the Karla caves, the historical Buddhist caves dating back to the second-century BC on the edge of the Deccan plateau and accessible from Lonavala on the road or railway station between Poona and Bombay.

For me that meant taking the Deccan Queen and the road out of Lonavala to Karla.

I took the urn with me and set out one morning from Poona railway station carrying it in a cloth shoulder-bag. A rickety tourist van took me and six others to Karla from Lonavala station. The other travellers, three of them hippies, one American and two Dutch, were interested in Buddhism and had read guides to the caves. I was on my own obscure mission, one which I, aged seventeen, didn't want to talk to my fellow travellers about.

I set out with the urn of ashes to find Karvanjilla and its river. I walked down the hill paths from Karla because I distinctly remembered Chandri saying that her village was not on the plains. Once out of range of the tourist field of Karla, the hills or mountains of the Western Ghats, the range that fringes the Deccan plateau and descends to the narrow western coastline of the vast southern Indian peninsula, looked green, forested and menacing from close and blue and grey and endless in the distance.

I must have walked two miles down and along the hills following a path where one or two could walk abreast till I came across some women working in a hilly field. I asked them where Karvanjilla was. They hesitated. They spoke to each other and then one of them pointed down the path I was already on. Their hesitation told me that they didn't know.

A few hundred yards on, I came across a man herding a few skinny goats and asked him.

He seemed to know the place immediately. He said I was to go back along the path I had come for two "phurlings" and then take the severe turn down into the valley. I wouldn't see

the village immediately, but when I went round the rump of the hill it would be below me. He gratuitously added that he lived in a village far above it.

I don't think he understood the exact length of a furlong to which he had referred. It was for him an arbitrary measure of distance, a way of saying "go along for a bit". Nevertheless I took the only path down the hill that I came across.

The rest of his directions couldn't be faulted. I did cross the shoulder of the hill and saw the village below me, not more than a collection of straw, wood and bamboo huts.

It must have taken me an hour to scramble down, sometimes losing the path and passing through dense forest from which I lost sight of the village or of where I was going. But I knew it was down.

I found it. There didn't seem to be any roads or lanes or discipline to the way the huts were scattered. There was certainly a clearing in which the huts were situated, and below the clearing, farmland of sorts carved out of the forests and the sudden scrub. A man attending to the yoke of a bullock cart sat in front of his hut smoking a bidi. I asked him if this was indeed Karvanjilla and he said it was. I asked him where the river was. He looked puzzled.

"What river, there's no river here," he said.

"A stream of some sort then?"

"No stream of any sort," he said. "If you're thirsty there's the well. There are ten wells in the village. No shortage of wells."

"So no flowing water?"

"Why do you come here asking questions? No one comes here. Where are you from?"

"Poona," I said, and he nodded as though that were an acceptable answer.

"Try the well there," he said.

I thanked him and walked through the village. So there was no river here. Why had Chandri told my mother that she wanted her ashes to be scattered in the river that ran by her village?

It was now late morning. Should I go back to Karla? I had walked to the end of the village and across a few fields. In the agricultural patch of the village's land I saw a bullock cart ambling along. It meant there must be a road or path of some sort, and I walked across the muddy fields. There was a road and another bullock cart came by.

"Where does the road lead?"

"To the main road," the cart-driver said.

"Are there cars on it?"

"Trucks even. Blow dust in your face and muddy the animals. Dreadful."

"How far is it?" I asked and immediately realized I wouldn't get any sort of accurate answer.

"Two hours." I saw him looking at his wrist, which sported a wristwatch, and he was looking at me to see if I had noted his valuable possession. "Hop on if you want to go there," he said.

I did. His estimate was fairly accurate. We reached the main road in a little over two hours because he hurried his bulls along, sticking his bamboo into their posteriors to make them move faster. He was obviously showing off to me. His cart was empty because he was going to fill it up with oil drums on the way back and this was downhill and fast. The return journey, he pointed out, would be tough on the animals, and they would earn their keep by dragging the cart uphill. I said I sympathized.

When we got to the highway he stopped his cart. He wasn't going on the highway but wished me good luck. I knew he would be insulted if I offered him money. He wanted to be doing the city fellow a country favour. Nevertheless I tried, saying I'd like to leave him a gift for his bulls. He smiled and said he was rich, much richer than I seemed to be, and he couldn't take tips from hitchhikers. I resigned myself and thanked him.

I flagged down a truck. It was going towards Bombay rather than back towards Poona, but I asked the driver whether he could drop me at a town where I could take a train back. He said he'd take me to Bombay if I wanted. I accepted.

In Bombay I made my way to Dadar station in the north, and I was in time to catch the evening's Deccan Queen back to Poona. I boarded it with my urn. I would scatter Chandri's ashes at the sangam, the confluence of the Moola and the Mootha in Poona.

Dusk fell as the train went inland to the foot of the hills and began the climb. I was sitting in a compartment with people who appeared to be regular commuters on the DQ as four of them had reserved seats and had set up a card game. The other passengers in the compartment sat behind them and peered at one or the other player's cards. They seemed to know each other and offered each other tea from thermos flasks.

As the train climbed the ghats before Khandala, it passed through various tunnels and came to a stop at a point called Monkey Hill, a station without a platform marked with a sign bearing its name.

The regulars, the commuters between Poona and Bombay, didn't seem perturbed. The old girl had whims, but would normally get them to and fro on schedule. They continued their card game. Someone made a joke that I didn't catch but their whole gathering laughed out loud.

It began to rain. Some instinct made me pick up my bag and take the urn out. I went to the door of the carriage and pushed the metal-framed glass shutter of the window up.

There were horizontal bars there preventing passengers from leaning out. The rain was light and pleasant on my hands as I stretched out.

The train began to move, and as it did I saw the mountain stream, no more than a little gutter by the side of the track. It had been enlivened by the rainfall. Here was Chandri's river, I thought, the idyllic little stream that would bear her ashes away, probably joining up with larger streams, which would cascade as waterfalls from some rocky promontory and then gurgle its way to the plains where it would join some sluggish river flowing into the Arabian Sea. This is where she would want her ashes to be, to flow with the currents of her mountains.

I took the cotton bung off the top of the urn and, turning round to make sure no one was looking, I projected the ashes as far as I could towards the stream at the side of the tracks. The ashes came out of the narrowing top of the vase in spurts as some of the unburnt bits of wood clogged its neck. Then it was empty. I stuffed the vase and the bung back in my pack and went back to my seat.

In a little more than an hour the DQ terminated at Poona railway station. The regulars waited near the doors, their timings synchronized with the train's arrivals and departures. I alighted after them, and as I passed them on the platform saw three of them at the window of the carriage we'd been in.

"I told you it was some idiot throwing ash," one of them said.

He ran his finger along the glass, and as I paused and watched, made a line in the coating on it.

"Some villager's campfire. They could set the whole bloody forest on fire, the vandals," another of them said as they walked to the exit.

"Thank God it rained a bit," the first man said.

"Good night, Savantji ... good night, Lulu sahib ... good night all ... See you in the morning ... Arrey bring one of your wife's Parsi onion omelettes, Lulu..."

The ticket collector at the exit knew them and let them pass. He stopped me and took my ticket, clicking his metal ticket-punching machine.

On the way home I weighed up the chances of a small fragment of Chandri's ashes not having been swept by the rain and wind on to the sides of the Deccan Queen and having as I innocently intended reached that little stream. A little piece of her should surely have gone to the turbulence of the resting place she desired.

⋆

(*My sister read* Deccan Queen *and writes... –fd*)

My dearest brother,

Just read your latest thing and loved every minute ... but that story about Chandri—what is wrong with you, are you getting Alzheimer's or what? OK, you may have been 2 or 3 years old when it happened but you must have heard a million times how Chandri on the train from Pakistan went to fill water, in those army water-bottles with felt on them, at the tap in a station where the train stopped and that you started crying and mother thought you needed fresh air and sent you out and how some fellow with a sword rushed on to the platform from the tracks where he had been walking and attacked you and how Chandri while defending you had her index finger slashed by the sword and it had to be amputated by the doctor after the fellow had been shot dead in the head by the army guards of the train.

You may not have the exact memory, but mother and father told the story a zillion times and at least you should have mentioned it.

And what's all this rubbish about the Deccan Queen? It was some slow mail train that you and I BOTH took from Bombay with her ashes and the damn thing stopped at every little station and places we didn't even know existed. I suppose you wanted to spice up your wretched story so you wrote the first thing that came into your head but you should have said at the beginning of the book that this is mostly fiction or just how you remember it or maybe that's the same thing but I hope it isn't because then all my memories of growing up would be only true because I thought they were true!

Big kiss,
Zazzoo

*

My Dear Zaz,

Gosh, didn't realize you'd turned philosopher in your old age or that you could write stream of consciousness. Too much JJ?—that's James Joyce—better known in Parsi circles as Jamshed Joycewalla…

And please don't talk rot, it wasn't her index finger that was damaged, it was the little finger of her left hand, and it happened when she fell off the train at night looking for water. At least that's what I remember Mum telling me. The stuff about her fighting a swordsman with her bare hands was, I remember her saying, made up by Daddy in one of his storytelling modes. If you remember when he elaborated on events one way or the other and everyone knew it was an elaboration. We all, Mum especially, kept it to ourselves because contradicting him would have served no purpose. And boy, he would have been furious at being contradicted and filled up on more whisky.

But maybe that's wrong. Maybe all the time, being Daddy's girl you believed every syllable of his stories.

Let's fight it out when we meet—hate to quarrel by e-mail.

Lots of xx
f

*

To the Editor by e-mail

Dear Sir/Madam,

Why do you give publicity to the lies my nephew Dhondy tells? He constantly makes himself older by three or four years so that he can say that he was present during the trauma of Partition. It is true that his father, my brother-in-law, was in Quetta at Partition, but the wretched boy was not even born then. He was comfortably born a year after Partition in Dr Bandorawalla's Nursing Home and we all went with presents for his mother, my elder sister.

Both he and his sister have been deluded by their late father into believing all this stuff because he too, though he was a very good man and I would never call him a liar, was very susceptible to exaggerating his stories and may have even told these children that they both lived through the horrors of Partition.

I can remember dinner parties when he used to entrance the guests with all this stuff and his adventures in the Second World War and about a friend of his who turned traitor to the Indian army and was found twenty years later still believing that the Second World War was not over.

But maybe that is not where your writer gets his stuff from. He must have just made it up. He just likes to show-off and write these silly articles claiming that he was born in what is now Pakistan and making his early years full of historical troubles. He has lived through no such thing. He should read a book called Midnight's People by Suleiman Roshtie which will tell him the real traumas of Partition instead of the pretending he is doing.

I mean him no malice but have always believed that printed material must be truthful, even though we know that the newspapers are full of lies.

Your obedient servant,
K.A. Antia
(Maternal uncle to Writer)

Choosing My Cloth

Down the street from our house in Poona there was an alley that went off the main street. We called the junction Narayan's corner because a blind beggar sat there day after day, from late afternoon through the evening into the night, on a coir mat with a metal plate before him, cymbals in one hand, clanging in rhythm to his song, which was no more than a repeated chant, one of the names of God: "Narayan, Narayan, Narayan-na."

There were no more lyrics to the song, and the cymbals provided the only relief from the entreating voice.

We teenagers used to gather at Narayan's corner till there were a sufficient number to proceed to the tea shops at the end of Mahatma Gandhi Road. Narayan had grown used to us. If one addressed him directly he would pause the chant. His eyelids would flutter over the discoloured pupil-less marble of his eyes. His mouth would be agape. He would let out a little cry if he heard the chink of a coin being deposited in his bowl. Thanks or disbelief. The more cruel and callous would go up to him and say, "Will you be an eyewitness to the accident yesterday?" Others would go further and ask him how he knew whom he was having sex with. His standard answer to all was to beg forgiveness. The questioners would put four annas in his bowl to demonstrate penitence and let Narayan know that among fellow fatalists there could be no hard feelings.

Blindness was a condition of our streets. We never asked Narayan how he had come to lose his eyesight or whether he was born without it. He was a fixture of our neighbourhood, and in an eerie way his voice, in the early dusk as I returned home walking or bicycling, was reassuring. He was chanting the name of his God. The world flowed by him.

He was there every day over the years as I passed through my teens.

On the last evening before I left Poona for Bombay to fly to London and to Cambridge University, I awaited my friends by Narayan's corner, and out of superstition and sentiment, I gave Narayan a five-rupee note, and not wanting it to blow out of his bowl, I put it in his hand.

"Who is it? Why?" he asked, unused to being given a paper note.

He was feeling its size to ascertain the denomination.

"I am going to Bombay tomorrow," I said.

He thought about it, his blind eyes blinking.

"Bombay! That's far away. I'll never get to see it," he said.

*

It was to Bombay I had to go to finalize my scholarship arrangements. The gateway to the uncharted, the unknown. The excitement of going abroad was permeated with dread.

Mrs Vesugarh was reputed to be a dragon, but a dragon who guarded the gates of promise I had fought valiantly to pass through. I had passed my college exams well and now had a Poona university degree. I had applied and then been summoned and, having gone through several interviews, had been granted a scholarship by the Tata Foundation for the Higher Education of Indians, an institution dedicated to paying for Indians to study abroad. It was a privilege given to a few who were informed after the suspense of applications and waiting for the result of interviews that they were among the chosen. There were twelve. It was common knowledge that there had been thousands of applicants.

From another corner of the country where my father was serving with troops on the northern frontier against Pakistan came his letter, briefly congratulating me and saying how happy and proud he was and then going on to admonish me about shaving my beard, wearing my shirt tucked into my trousers and not spouting the Marxist and existential jargon that he characterized as the passing conceits of my adolescence. I mustn't go before my benefactors as anything but a well brought-up young man. It was a sweet but severe letter, and his desperate concern saturated every sentence.

My father was a military man and expressed himself in commands, but somewhere between the lines he was proposing a truce and asking me to bow, for once, to his experience of life. I had carried on the minor rebellion of manners, our version of the generation gap, forming my own styles and ambitions and cultivating the air of being intellectually contemptuous of his. But his letter brought me to the senses I didn't think I possessed.

Suppose he was right? Suppose the directors of the Tata Foundation and this Mrs Vesugarh who was reputed to scrutinize every potential scholar with ferocity, took one look at this bearded youth and decided to cancel the scholarship? The whole dream of escape, escape from India, escape to a wider world, so vital, even desperate now, would vanish. They had the power to say "no, that was not it at all, that was not what we wanted at all..."

I shaved my wispy beard. I was nineteen. I shone my shoes, I wore a crisp white shirt and my uncle dropped me at Flora Fountain, the old colonial official district of Bombay, fifteen minutes before my appointment.

In the year before, having quit Bombay and the Department of Chemical Technology, I had returned to Poona, a refusenik and a failure, and had fallen in love. Mala, seventeen years old, who had made my life worth living, and whom I was nevertheless planning to abandon for three years at a British university, had come to Bombay with me. She would look at the shops while I was undergoing my final scrutiny, and she'd be at an appointed place on the pavement in an hour. What's more, her mother, who was rich, beautiful, a Bombay society hostess and tolerant of our assumedly unconsummated relationship, would send the chauffeur and car to wait for us in the car park at Flora Fountain.

In all my years I had never enquired who Flora was and why she had a fountain in the official centre of Bombay, but passing her that morning as I crossed the square to judgement, I prayed to her as the nearest deity. I was a socialist atheist, but a little prayer for luck wouldn't hurt.

In the building that housed the Tata Foundation, I was shown into a vast room with a single desk behind which sat Mrs Vesugarh. She must have been in her seventies, with a wrinkled and severe face. My first impression was that she looked like Bertrand Russell. I was announced and asked in, and I shook the hand she distractedly offered me. She was familiar with the notes I had written and the comments of those of her cohorts who had conducted the previous interviews.

"Why Cambridge, Mr Dhondy?"

"I did apply to American universities and, as I said in my application, to Lumumba University in Russia, but they ask you to spend two years studying Russian."

"Yes, but you chose Cambridge, England." She was impatient. "Why does one go to Oxford or Cambridge?"

I was sitting opposite her, across her vast desk, neat but crowded with files, my mind racing. This wasn't chit-chat.

"Because they have the best brains on most subjects," I volunteered.

"That's all nonsense. You go to Oxford or Cambridge to make contacts that you can call upon for the rest of your life. That's all."

"Yes, ma'am," I said meekly. Who was I to contradict her?

"Now, Mr Dhondy, you see that door there? Behind that door is a toilet. Go and use it."

Her tone was commanding, and there was no smattering of mischief in it. I didn't understand the nature of the test. Was I supposed to protest, to ask a question, to make a joke?

I decided to obey. I went to the door and to the toilet as one does if a doctor asks you for a sample. She was looking at a newspaper when I re-emerged and sat down.

We talked about why I had chosen to read natural sciences. She recalled her time at Oxford in the early century.

"You must be wondering what that was all about?" she eventually asked, indicating the little door.

"I was," I said.

"I wanted to hear if you flushed after going," she said.

I thanked my stars, or Flora of the fountain, that I had not panicked and neglected to do it.

"We chose twelve of you this year. You shall meet some of them. Do you know how many applicants we had, Farrukh?"

She was using my first name. I had passed the test.

"I have no idea, ma'am, but the letter did say … er … a lot."

"Seventy thousand," she said. "All wanting money to study something somewhere." She shook her head and waved her hand in a gesture that said it was hopeless, that she had to turn all of them down.

A secretary knocked and came in to announce that the tailor was here. The tailor and his assistant, carrying bales of woollen cloth, came in. Mrs Vesugarh was expecting them.

"I've decided we're going to equip you with a tweed jacket, a pair of Oxford bags and a suit, Farrukh. The tailor will measure you, and you'll come back here in five days for a fitting so I can look you over. Now choose your cloth."

The assistant had deposited the bales on a table. The tailor, a caricature with his bald head, a measuring tape draped over his shoulders and a Dickensian ledger and pencil in his hand, was all smiles. He had been Mrs V's wardrobe man for years, presumably outfitting generations of scholars. He began to boast about it, remembering which famous scholar had chosen which length of material. Mrs V looked very severely at him and he stopped.

Now I had to choose. It was an era of change. The Beatles were smashing the skylight of the charts. British youth featured in everything I read as Mods or Rockers, all long hair, kempt or unkempt, leather jackets, drainpipes. Oxford bags? A tweed jacket and a suit?

I was leafing through the bales of Indian tweed, but Mrs Vesugarh had already chosen for me.

"I think this check and this grey for the trousers. Yes?"

I said I thought they were perfect. She had come out from behind her desk, a diminutive dynamo of a figure in her silk brocade sari with a heavily embroidered gold and silver border. She had been decisive about the jacket and bags and now she drew back.

"What shall we have for a suit, Farrukh?" she asked. I pulled a bale from the pile.

"That's quite nice," I said.

She took it contemptuously from my hands and cast it aside. "Mr Dhondy, no gentleman wears a brown suit!"

I wanted to say I wasn't really thinking, that I had made a mistake, but she had pronounced and moved on. She was choosing a dark blue. I said it was the one I really had in mind. I was measured, approved, sent away.

Mala and the car were waiting for me. She looked at me questioningly, some faint hope that we could stay together in her query. No, it had gone well. I told her about the interview and the clothes. Yes, I was going. She—we—would have to bear the separation. We sat in silence.

"Let's drop the chauffeur and you drive, we'll drive out. I want to spend the last few days with you, alone with you," she said.

"There's not much chance in either of our houses," I said.

"Then let's catch the DQ back to Poona this evening," she said. "At last we'll have four hours together, and then we can spend the night at your aunts' and come back in the morning because I know you have all this scholarship and clothes and rubbish to do."

We went and it was as she said. We sat in the open doorway on the floor of the third-class carriage and looked at the stars as the train traversed the ghats.

In the morning we were back in Bombay, and I had a set of car keys to one of her mother's cars having asked the chauffeur to leave it in the station car park overnight.

"Just drive through the city. Through Bhendi Bazaar and the crowded bits. I don't want to go home. I'd rather be stuck with you in a traffic jam," she said.

I drove into the heart of the city from the station plaza.

And true to her wishes, we got stuck in an hour-long traffic jam in which every vehicle fought for each inch of space, advancing against the next man's fender. Horns blasted, tempers frayed, the cars advanced to the bottleneck on Princess Street, four unruly streams trying to resolve themselves into one.

"I don't mind this at all," she said. "Patience with a purpose."

"I don't feel that philosophic," I said. "We could have gone to a coffee bar or sat on the beach."

A taxi driver, obviously contemptuous of "privates" as he called all cars that weren't for hire, couldn't match the initial acceleration of my smooth Japanese car with which I beat him by micro-seconds into a two-foot gap. He leaned out of his open window and cast the foulest aspersions on the sexual propriety of my mother and sisters. Irony would be better than abuse, I decided. I leaned through my window.

"*Cycle ka licence hai*?" I asked. "Did he have a license to even ride a bicycle?"

"*Arrey chal chal, betey, teri maa ka*..." he began.

He had used the word "betey", son, and I fastened on to it.

"*Kis ko beta kehta hai, gandoo*?" I shouted, my street lore returning from memory—"Who are you calling 'sonny', you bum-boy?" And then, "*Chaltey reh. Terey oomar key merey betey Singapore mein ricksha challatey hein,*"—"Get going, I have kids as old as you pushing rickshaws in Singapore".

I thought I had administered the coup de grace. Mala put on her large dark glasses and, ignoring our shouting match, looked every bit the contemptuous memsahib who was allowing her chauffeur to fight it out with the hoi polloi. My antagonist kept his engine running but stepped out of his cab and came threateningly round it to me. The traffic was stationary. Mala pretended nothing was happening. He'd kick my head in now. I must brazen it out. I stuck my elbow out of the open window. He came to it all smiles, with an extended hand.

"*Aap Singapore key ho? Mein bhi Singapore ka hoon*!" he said, enthusiasm and fellow-feeling darting out of his eyes. "You are from Singapore? So am I!"

I shook his hand. I wasn't about to explain that I was using the word Singapore as symbolic of parental abandonment and eastern vice and not as a real place. The irony was stillborn. He was greeting me in the desert of Bombay as a co-citizen of the oasis of memory: Singapore. I was to go to lunch. His wife could cook Malaysian curry.

"Your madam doesn't mind me speaking to you, does she?" he asked.

"No, no, no. She's a very lenient employer," I said.

"Madam, let him follow right behind me through the traffic; I will cut out a path through these motherfuckers who shouldn't be allowed on the roads," he said to her.

She gave him a broad smile. Behind the dark glasses she was enjoying this.

Then the taxi man scribbled an address on some remnant of a grubby receipt, a ten-line address in Hindi and with one or two words in English, with instructions on how to get to his humble dwelling, while the traffic hooted and screamed around us. He then crumpled the address he had written up. I would never find his house in the slums of Bombay, but if I met him in the porch of the Taj Hotel at nine at night the next day, he would take me with him.

"You can finish your shift by then?" he asked.

"Of course he can," Mala replied.

I assured him I'd be there. The jam had cleared and horns were blowing. He was a burly fellow wearing a vest that hung off his belly. He got into his cab and drove, waving, ahead of me, ploughing a furrow for me to follow through the traffic, and then at the next corner he disappeared into the anonymity of the city.

Singapore? I had never been east of Calcutta. I had said it as one says "Timbuktu", never thinking that the actual will one day challenge the symbolic.

I didn't go to the porch of the Taj the next day. Perhaps he turned up, perhaps he waited. I had named a city and the name was a joke to me but a memory to him. Singapore. I felt guilty, guilty for not turning up, wasting his evening, wasting his wife's curry—guilty of the sin of callous irony. I thought about them. He would put it down to the indifference of the prosperously employed, to the callousness of those who didn't have to earn a living driving cabs. He wouldn't have analysed the rhetoric and concluded that a fellow in his mid-twenties couldn't possibly have children pushing rickshaws in Singapore. We hear what we want to hear and disregard the rest.

We did go to a coffee bar and then we did sit on the beach and watch the tide come in.

*

(*A blogger who says he is Dutch appends this comment to the e-version of this story. –fd*)

Mumbai—symbol, metaphor, parable, launching pad, dream, hell, home, hiding place, graveyard, nepenthe, joke, but certainly Jekyll and Hyde.

We came and went on the Deccan Queen.

Just a city of filthy streets and boredom.

Unlike Singapore with clean streets and boredom.

Mumbai, no Big Apple—more Big Rotting Aubergine.

Why was Babylon abandoned?

The Timbuktus of fable and absurdity have become real with the troops of Mali and France fighting latter-day Mahdis for a piece of the desert, for a piece of future.

@LavrentiSpec

(Miriam – this piece of correspondence could go in as a story on its own, n'est-ce pas? – *fd*)

Avalanche

From: Anilhitfilms32@gmail.com

Mr Dhondy Sir,

I have been reading your fine book *Deccan Queen* and was so jealous when I first saw the title, speaking frankly, because I was myself writing one with the same name. You have beaten me to it and I was very struck and disturbed till I bought and read the same.

I was overcome with relief when I found that yours is not a real story but like a diary with your grandfather and uncles and everything. Mine, you see, is a story and I have been writing the first three chapters. I must confess that I am not a seasoned book writer as I have regular employment writing Hindi scripts for films and all my time is taken up therein. What little I have to spare I want to devote to the much more august task of authoring literature.

I will not even think that I am reaching the standards set by persons of your ability in any way. I am even humbly confiding that I am a little nervous in writing this e-mail to you and asking a favour that you read my first chapters and tell me what good advice you have to give the like of aspiring writers such as myself.

My excuse for this bold venture is that some of my efforts at writing in Hindustani language for Hindi Movie producers and directors have been somewhat successful and even some hits. You might have heard of the films in which I have this above-mentioned screenwriting hand are the following:

Rasta: a film about the end of the world where a father and young son are braving all the dangers with wild persons and animals still roaming and attacking.

Mausam ki Raat ka Sapna: a story in which four lovers are in a forest where two of them are running away to have love marriage instead of arranged marriage as per her father's wish. A lot of changings take place in the forest inspired by magicians and people with power over spells and there is some royal interest also.

Crorepati Ladka: this was a very big hit with Kunal playing Puppoo, the boy who grows up. When he is too young he is living in the seaside village and one night near the burning ghats he is assaulted by a runaway prisoner who asks him for help with food and breaking chains. The young boy is threatened and very much frightened and so is doing what the prisoner who is an escapee is asking. The prisoner is captured by police once more and taken away and then the young man grows up and is still in a poor farmer job when a lawyer is coming to his village and saying that he is now a crorepati, a millionaire because someone is secretly sending him money to make him into a sahib.

He must go to Mumbai where he will have a house and servants and cars. There is a lot of love story too with an old lady whose husband was run away on her marriage day and she has just kept her house with all the rotting sweetmeats and fireworks exactly like the day her heart was break. This old lady has bring up a girl adopted by her and teached her to break heart of man just like she was subjected to. Our hero, Puppoo, falls in love with this heartless girl and even when he has a lot of money she cannot devote herself to him. Then he finds that the person who has left him the money is the prisoner to whom he gave food and escape route when he was a boy. The film had silver and golden jubilee in Mumbai and in Kolkata and was even dubbed in Tamil.

Mr Dhondy, I can send you other films also of mine which were hits but you must be having enough of this so I will forbear.

Hope you agree for reading my humble efforts at *Deccan Queen* chapters.

Your friend of the future,
Anil Golchand

*

From: prisonerofpoona@gmail.com

Dear Anil Golchand,

I am sure you should finish writing your *Deccan Queen* and send it to a publisher. I must confess I haven't seen any of the films you outline, but then I live in London and am not a great film-goer. Reading your outlines, I don't think I am competent to criticize your chapters or be of use in any way. Perhaps you can think of changing the name of your book so it isn't confused with mine and people don't pick up what I have written expecting what will undoubtedly, on the evidence of your film-outlines, be dramatic and popular.

Yours ever,
Farrukh Dhondy

*

From: Anilhitfilms33@gmail.com

Dear Mr Dhondy,

Please note first my change of e-mail address, even though I am keeping previous one alive as people maybe haven't taken note of this latest one which is keeping in time with events because my film *Cockroachman* has become my 33rd big hit. It is as you might have heard a combination between horror and superhero and also has a social message which is that even a despised creature like a cockroach, which people are hating very much, can be the model for a man who becomes a hero by smashing crimes and fighting evil while dressing and behaving in cockroach fashions to disguise from criminals who are always after him.

I am thankful for your neat and kind reply but must tell you I think you are mistaken. I am convinced and other people whose advice I have been asking are also similar in their opinion that YOU will be the best person to read my four chapters and say even a few words in helpful guidance. I will not burden you with them of course till you make a wholehearted consent to taking this trouble for me.

By the way I hope you will not be offended if I ask you why you have adopted the puzzling e-mail ID of prisonerofpoona?

Your friend,
Anil Golchand

*

From: prisonerofpoona@gmail.com

Dear Anil Golchand,

Congratulations on your success with *Cockroachman*. Yes, I have seen the posters on a brief visit to a literary festival in Mumbai and have even heard that it will be released in London.

As for your book *Deccan Queen* I really feel it's unfair to put pressure on me to read your chapters and am sincerely volunteering the opinion that my reading may not be helpful.

As for my e-mail ID, it is the only one I use. It simply means that some of my memory as a writer remains imprisoned though not entombed in the environs and ghosts of my childhood in that city.

Yours ever,
Farrukh Dhondy

*

From: Anilhitfilms33@gmail.com

Dear Mr Dhondy,

I don't know if you are just being shy or being stubborn. Forgive me if even thinking things like that offends you.

OK, I won't send you the five chapters I have written but at least tell me if the outline I am sending in a few lines reads for you as something that publishing companies in England and United States will jump up at. If you like it please feel free to send it to publishers of your choice and surely when it is a hit, I will never forget your services and kindness.

This is my story:

The Deccan Queen is running full one morning on its journey to Mumbai from Pune. On the train in first class is one expert learned detective whose name is Mr Harkishan Purohit. In the first class he gets talking to a man who says to him that he himself is a millionaire but he is far from happy because on that very train he is in great danger from a lot of people who want to kill him for different reasons. When the detective gets out to have a cup of tea at Lonavala station, he returns to find the man he spoke with having multiple woundings by which means he is murdered and so dead. Now because the train has started the police can't be called and as it is leaving Khandala and progressing down the winding way of the track down the mountainous ghats, a big rock-fall is taking place. The rock-fall stops the train and it is impossible for any immediate continuance of the journey. The rocks fall before, on and after the train so locking it in completely. Now Mr Purohit sets out to find who the murderer is.

He very soon finds out that the man who is killed is not the millionaire person he was claiming himself to be. He is in fact a criminal man who has been accomplice, still absconding, of a fellow who kidnapped a young child in Kolkata and then murdered the child. Both parents of the child are dead.

Mr Purohit unleashes the fact that plenty people want to kill that accomplice fellow but nobody on that Deccan Queen is really who they say they are. My hero is stuck inside a dark jungle of lies and deception and then has to find some ray of light and discover the murderer.

I hope this much story has made you curious at least to know the rest.

I remain hopeful of a favourable reply.

Please revert promptly out of kindness to an anxious fan of yours.

Your friend and fan,
Anil Golchand

*

From: prisonerofpoona@gmail.com

Dear Anil Golchand,

For a man busy with screenplay writing for the innovative and original industry of Bollywood, you seem to have a lot of time to read English literature. Or perhaps you borrow the DVDs of books that have been filmed and watch them with your finger on the fast-forward button so as to steal plots from Dickens, Shakespeare and even, unexpectedly, Cormac McCarthy.

I very much doubt, on reading your outline which is something of a homage to Ms Agatha Christie, sole author and inventor of *Murder on the Orient Express*, that any western publisher will touch the work, even if they have sub-editors keen to correct the English.

I am surprised that Bollywood and you and your producers get away with such blatant violations of copyright.

Please don't write again.

F. Dhondy

*

From: Anilhitfilms33@gmail.com

Dear Dhondy,

I don't know which is greater, your pompose reply to me or your stupid ignorants about the copyrighting laws. There is no copywrights, my friend, in a story. Dickens and Shakespeare are dead and they were in any case stealing their stories from Bocassto, Blutack and other Italian and German writers.

You are insulting my films without even looking at them. In Hindi we have a proverb for people like you: "The jealous fox says grapes he can't reach are sour."

My book, and I am not changing title please note, will sell thousand times more than your stupid personal nonsense.

As for you telling about my English, please see I know some good English: Fuck off!

Anil33hits.

On Avon

All those crossings. Are we ever transformed? Isn't the talk of being a new person hot air?

I am years away from school and college and the India I grew up in. I work now in a TV company in London, a delightful job, if you can call it that, commissioning programmes and bringing them to the screen.

I walk into my office on the seventh floor one evening after a hard edit and Eva, my secretary, brings in a hand-delivered letter.

"This character wanted to see you and he waited a couple of hours, but then he had to go so he left this note," she said.

"What character?"

"Never seen him before. He was at the reception, and I told him you'd be in later. He really waited."

"What did he want? Flogging some programme idea? You should have asked him to write in."

"'course I did. That's probably it."

I opened the envelope. It had a brief hand-written note:

Dear Farrukh,

I'm a fan of yours from way back and would really appreciate it if you would come and see this production of the Royal Shakespeare Company's *Coriolanus* in which I play a part. Hope this is not an unwelcome intrusion or impudence.

Yours ever,
Dick Richards

I searched my mind but concluded I didn't know any Dick Richards. Two of the best tickets in the house were enclosed, paper-clipped to the note.

"Good idea?" Eva asked.

"Not an idea, an invitation from some guy I don't know. But this is the show that's got those fantastic reviews."

"What show?"

"Stratford production of *Coriolanus*."

"Yeah, I done the cuttings. I saw this geezer, Richard Dick who does, like, the lead role."

"I think you'll find it's Dick Richards."

"Same difference," says Eva.

"Do you know 'same difference' doesn't mean what you think it means? What you meant was there is *no* difference, whereas the phrase 'same difference' can only be applied to a similar interval between two quantities, such as 'the difference between five and seven is the same as between seven and nine'."

"Yeah, wha'ever! You do go on, Dolly," Eva says, using the name "Dolly Daydreams" she has adopted for me since she came in one morning and found me sleeping under the desk in my office. I hadn't been home as I'd been in an edit room till five and then had appointments early the next day. Such was that work and life.

"Sorry. Will you book a double room in Stratford for that night and a couple of train tickets for the morning returning next day? I think I'll go. And I think I know who'll want to go with me."

"I'll check your diary. Up to tricks, Dolly?"

"Please! I meant my daughter who's doing the play for A levels."

"Yeah, yeah," says Eva and then, "You can't go. You got to go to a Board meeting that evening."

"Boring. Send my apologies."

I travel to Stratford and book into the twin room with my daughter.

"You got us one room?" she asks. She's seventeen and values her teen privacy.

"Twin beds."

"Yes, but you snore!"

"Use earplugs. And show some decent gratitude. I've dodged important meetings and pulled several strings to get into this sell-out show."

"Why do you lie? Eva told me some geezer sent you them for free and you hadn't even thought about it till then."

"That's as may be, but no one can prove or disprove what I had or had not thought about. The mind is a private dimension."

"You do talk a lot of rot, Dad."

I left her to dress and went down to the bar.

They were among the best seats in the house. Coriolanus, none other than Dick Richards as the programme told us, came on. It must have taken me ten minutes into the play to recognize, to identify the voice and the postures under the changed frame and the cultivated accent and the hair dyed black to play an authentic Roman.

Golly McKay.

The performance was as convincing as several reviews had said it was. At one moment, as he addressed the audience from the front of the stage, I fancied he was looking towards the seats he had reserved to see if I was there. He may have discerned an outline in the darkness of the auditorium, but would he know me now if he saw me in the street?

Even before the curtain calls were over a stagehand rushed to our seats and handed me a scribbled note: "Stupendous! Backstage and dinner and champagne. Please!"

Had he scribbled it in the wings while waiting for his cue after he'd ascertained that I was there?

*

I had booked a table in our hotel dining room that evening, but Golly insisted that for old times' sake we eat an Indian meal and said he knew just the place. It was a curry house called The Deccan Queen and he intended to spring the name on me as a surprise. The manager and waiters knew him well.

"Mr Dicks, always best table for you," they said and without him ordering it they brought a bottle of their best red wine.

"Mr Dicks is loving this wine we are keep specially for him," the manager said. "He give us this lucky name."

Golly explained to my daughter and me. He had poked his nose into the High Street property when it was just being decorated as a restaurant. He was playing small parts in repertoire with the company at the time. He had told the owner who he was and explained that he had a lifelong connection and indeed a generational connection to India. His father had inaugurated the famous train that ran from Bombay to Poona.

The proprietor had heard of the Deccan Queen and when Golly passed by a few days later he accosted him and said their partnership committee had decided to change the designated name from "Star of Bengal" to "Deccan Queen" and they hoped that he, as a famous actor, would bring his friends there.

Golly said he certainly would, and when the restaurant opened under the proud name it did so with a sign in the window that said:

"Excellent and Authentic Cuisine"
Signed Dick Richards

Golly protested that he hadn't ever uttered those words but the proprietor grinned and said, "But you will think so for our sakes."

The meal was muck but Golly told my daughter that it was far better than what we used to get from the kitchens of our school in Poona. As the evening progressed and he came back to the hotel for a drink in the bar, my daughter went up to sleep.

I asked about his brothers. They were doing well.

"Let me tell you something else, Farrukh; another trick of fate."

"All ears," I said.

"A colonial story lingering on. You know I left school and India with Shakespearana. We went in the first few months that I was with them to Australia, and in Brisbane a lady approached me after a performance. It was *Two Gentlemen of Verona*. 'Your stage name is Richard Richard but I am told by Mr Kendall that your real name is Richard McKay,' she said. She wanted to talk to me about my family. I was somewhat reluctant. I'd changed my name to hide facts I didn't want to discuss.

"'Was your mother Kincaid Elliot?' the woman asked me.

"'She was,' I said.

"'She ran away to India with a railway fellow and lost touch with our family,' the lady said.

"'Your family?'

"'Yes, our family. She was my second cousin, and I never met her, I was younger, but had always heard that she had gone to India with an engineer or something of the sort. Her parents didn't approve of the match. You see, I don't know if you know, but your mother was of aristocratic stock. They owned lands and our relatives were titled—descended from Sir John Elliot.'

"All this was very strange to me. Neither my mother nor father had ever spoken of their elopement or of her background. All I knew was that they were both Scots.

"'So where is Mr McKay now? I know they didn't return to Scotland or England, but are they still in India? I should have asked, are they both alive?' the lady asked.

"I didn't know what I should say.

"'We don't care about your father, but the fact is that her relatives—she had no brothers and her sister left two sons—her nephews have been longing to trace her.'

"'Why?'

"'Because she was left money in her parents' wills, and they are finally the trustees of it. My husband and I live in Australia but we know that they are still looking for her. They knew that she had children through vague reports from people who returned from India but by now they presumed she was dead,' this lady said.

"'No. She's alive,' I said.

"She grasped my wrist as though we were on stage.

"I then told her that my father was a drunkard and a derelict and he had left my mother years ago. She asked me where she was now. I told her. I told her also that I had just begun to earn some money but as soon as I collected even a small sum, I would go back to Poona and get her out of that prison, that hellhole, even if she didn't know who I was. I told her that I prayed to God every night to keep her alive for long enough for me to get her away from there and heal her mind and body as best I could. I said I was saving every rupee I earned. That it was tearing me apart even after a few weeks of being away from Poona because I couldn't help her. I was helpless. I said my brother would help when he was earning, but he had also just finished school and would find a job. She asked if our dad had paid for our upbringing and I had to confess we lived on the charity of the Church and the generosity of the teachers.

"She was quite startled and moved by what I told her. She said we must phone my mother's nephews and their wives and tell them all this and she was sure they'd fly out to meet me and to rescue my mother.

"I didn't know whether I was dreaming, Farrukh. The lady took me to her mansion of a house and immediately phoned Scotland, told them what I had told her and put me on the phone. I was speaking to my Scottish cousin and after listening to my story he agreed to meet me in Bombay as soon as I could get someone to replace me on this run of *Two Gentlemen*. I explained to the company and flew to Bombay the next day.

"My cousin Edward and I took, yes, the Deccan Queen to Poona. Of course mother didn't know us. I don't even want to recall the state in which we found her. There were papers to sign and oaths to swear before solicitors and we paid a few bribes but in twenty-four hours Mum was in a hotel with us, completely confused but clean and well fed, with a haircut from the hotel's stylist and dressed in new clothes and shoes.

"Her eyes were empty, and I sat for hours gazing into them and hoping they'd fill up. She'd smile vaguely now and then. The corners of her mouth would tremble with the smile, and I didn't know whether they would go down in sorrow or curl upward with some recollection. Yes, she smiled. On the fourth day she began to talk. She wouldn't sleep the first few nights but then she did. I told her I was Richard and we were taking her away from the dreadful place where she had spent the years since Dougy was born and soon after Dad had had her committed to the madhouse.

"Soon, I told her she would be 'home'. Would she know the country she'd left as a girl? On the fifth day, she reached her hand out and touched my cheek. Man, I was crying. I went to school and told Mr Appleby everything and brought Dougy out of school to see Mum.

"Jamie had just left on an oil tanker from Bombay, and we tried to reach him by telegram. He had finished school with great exam results in the same year as me, though he's two and half years younger, and he was off to learn things about shipping oil. Dougy didn't remember Mum, but cousin Ned said we were going to take him out of school and take him back to Scotland with us.

"We left Bombay with Mum and went by air to London. I had told Mr Kendall why I wanted leave and that I would love to rejoin them as soon as I saw Mum home to Scotland. He was kind and more than understanding.

"We went through London to Aberdeen to their estate with several houses and properties in the vast grounds. Mum was to have, and to this day has, thirty years later, she's eighty now you know, a personal ayah. She now lives in one of the houses, and we visit her and she knows who we are and she speaks in the Scottish accent she left behind.

"Ned made me sign several papers that the family lawyers had drawn up and from the very first day they got their GP in to recommend psycho or brain treatment or whatever it was she needed. They were fantastic, yaar.

"She now remembers things in snatches and she laughs, she says, 'Just as I am beginning to remember things, oh dear, I am losing my memory and they are no longer there to be remembered.'

"Dougy is with her, and he and his Scottish wife have taken charge of my cousin's farm.

"I went back to India where the Company was touring and we went all over Asia and Australia and then old man Kendall fell ill. And Shakespearana was no more. I came back to Britain.

"Then I started acting here and there, old man. And here I stand. Or sit!"

His eyes were wet.

"That's so wonderful. Is it thirty years? Shit! I remember crying with you when we heard about your mother. So to which aristocratic family do your mother and the Elliots belong?"

"Old India-hands, Farrukh," Golly said. "You remember I once wrote in an exam for that idiot Bal John that they built roads and resthouses, dug wells and planted shady trees for travellers?"

"How could I forget? There we were writing essays about legislative reform in the Raj. Didn't you get whipped?"

"Well, it turns out my mother is descended from Lord Minto, Viceroy of India and joint author of the Morley-Minto reforms. Balls to all that legislative crap and your great intellectual answers. He was my ancestor and I say he dug wells and planted shady trees for travellers."